MW01094599

SHATTERED PIECES

A Heathens Ink Novel

By K.M.Neuhold

CONTENTS

SYNOPSIS

I was sure my heart had withered away years ago, but then you smiled at me, and I felt it beat again.

Years ago, I fell in love with my best friend's little brother. Then, he took his own life, leaving me shattered and unable to piece my heart back together. I've been a zombie for nine long years. Until a crazy, gorgeous man walked into Heathens Ink and injected color back into my world of gray. No matter how hard I try to resist Beck, he just won't give up on me. I would need steel willpower to withstand his gorgeous long legs in those high heels and his drawer full of lacy lingerie. But is this just a kinky hook up or does it have the possibility for more?

**Shattered Pieces is the fourth book in the Heathens Ink series, each book in the series CAN be read as a standalone. This is an steamy and emotional M/M romance with a guaranteed HEA

COPYRIGHT

Book and Cover design Natasha Snow Designs

DEDICATION

To two of my very favorite people in the world who both happen to be named Michelle. Michelle Slagan for being an amazing PA and for all the inspiring pics of beautiful men in lace. I didn't even know I had that fetish until you showed me the way. And to Michele Notaro for talking me off the many ledge. And to all my amazing beta readers and my incredible editor Rebecca J. Cartee and my proofreader Vicky for helping to make Gage's story as amazing as it deserves to be. And of course to my Nerds, you all are the wind beneath my wings and all that shit.

For extra enjoyment, here's my Shattered Pieces playlist on Spotify, get your tissues ready!

CHAPTER 1

Gage

They say time heals all wounds. What an absolute crock of shit.

Some wounds fester and ooze. Some wounds become more painful with each passing day until you can't remember what it felt like not to live in constant agony.

Nine fucking years since the love of my life killed himself. Nine excruciating years and I still see his face every time I close my eyes. I still reach for him in my sleep.

Gage Vaus died the same day Johnny Truman did. I've been nothing more than a walking zombie ever since.

"Your jokes are seriously the worst," I hear Nox complain from down the hall of Heathens Ink.

Eight years ago, my best friend, Adam, bought this building with the intent to turn it into his own tattoo shop. Adam also happened to be Johnny's older brother, and before Johnny's death, Adam and I had planned to open this place together, as joint owners. But when this opportunity arose only a year after we lost Johnny, I wasn't in a position to be a joint owner. I could hardly manage to make it through each day, let alone take on the responsibility of owning a business. I was there for Adam as much as I was able, though, and over time, I found working here and helping him build the business became my solace and a reason to wake up each day. I put my heart into it with him, and even though he's technically the sole owner, we both know our joint blood, sweat, and tears built Heathens.

"Shut up, you love my stupid jokes," Adam argues back affectionately.

A knife twists in my gut. Last night my world turned upside down when I walked in on my best friend naked and kissing our roommate, Nox. Not that I don't want Adam to be happy, and I'm the last one to be weird about a guy having a boyfriend. The thing is, in the almost thirty years I've known Adam, he never thought to mention to me that he's into guys.

My heart aches with the betrayal of knowing the person I've been closest to my entire life has been lying to me.

And underneath the hurt and betrayal, a fresh wave of loneliness ebbs and flows just beneath the surface.

I would never begrudge him anyone who can make him smile the way Nox does. But it feels like lately I'm surrounded by nothing but happy couples here at the shop. First, Madden found his knight in shining armor in a gorgeous and protective fireman who saved his life. Then Royal hit the jackpot, not only making the transition from best friends to boyfriends with Nash, the man he'd been pining after for years, but they also managed to integrate a third man who is so perfect for both of them. Then Nox showed up and turned Adam's world upside down.

Here I sit, alone as ever with no end in sight. At least Dani and Owen are both still single so I'm not the only sad sack left at Heathens.

The bell over the front door tinkles. I'm guessing it's my noon appointment here a little early, so I set aside my sketch book and heave myself out of my chair.

There's a man standing by the front desk. His back is to me, and I take note of his lithe frame and round, perky ass. But my heart isn't in it.

He turns around and my breath catches. He's absolutely stunning with every one of his eye-catching features highlighted by perfectly done makeup. His high cheekbones are slightly shimmery and bronzed, his pouty lips are an enticing shade of almost purple red, and his steel gray eyes with eyelashes a mile long are made up in what I've heard Dani refer to as 'smoky cat eye'. If I still had a type, this man would be exactly it.

He smiles, and I shake myself out of my reverie. I don't care how on point this dude's makeup is or how long his eyelashes are. He's not Johnny.

"Can I help you?"

He looks me up and down with interest, and

then a slow smile spreads over his lips.

"I'm sure you can."

His voice is a little deeper than I expected from his femme appearance. Sort of smooth and rich like expensive scotch.

"Are you my peacock tattoo appointment?" I prompt, part of me hoping he's a piercing walk-in so I can pass him off to Dani and forget about him all together.

"Yes."

I nod and head behind the counter to grab the sketch I made based on the conversation we had via email. When he contacted me through the website asking about having a colorful peacock done, I was immediately interested. I've always enjoyed color work and looking at him now, I think with his deeper skin tone, the colors I chose will turn out stunning.

"How does this look?" I ask, offering him the drawing.

His expression brightens further, and my stomach flutters. Maybe I'm coming down with something. Food poisoning probably.

"It's perfect," he sighs, reaching out to touch the drawing.

"Glad you like it. Let's head back to my work space and get started." I wave him toward the back of the shop. "I didn't catch your name during our email exchange."

"Beck. *Not* short for Beckham, short for Becket."

"Nice to meet you Not-Beckham. I'm Gage."

"Gage," he taps his index finger against his chin and inspects me again. "I like it; it suits you."

"I'm glad you approve," I laugh, surprising myself.

I motion him toward my tattoo chair once we're in my area, and I can't stop myself from noticing the fluid way his body moves.

The unbidden image pops into my mind of how he might swivel and move riding my dick.

My skin prickles with heat at the thought.

"Where do you want this?"

"On my left arm," he says, rolling up his sleeve.

"So, does the peacock mean something?" I ask as I prep Beck's skin.

The happiness in his eyes dims, and his lips tug down in a slight frown. I immediately regret the question. I would regret anything that steals the smile from his face. Beck has a face made for happiness, not sorrow.

"It's to remind me of my sister," he says after a few seconds. His tone doesn't welcome any further discussion on the topic so I let it go.

"You have any other ink?" I always like to know if I'm going to have a newbie freak out on my hands once the needle touches his skin.

"No. Is it going to hurt?" he asks. My attention snags on the way he nibbles his lush bottom lip anxiously.

"The outline will be the worst part, so if you

want to rest after that we can fill in the color another day," I suggest.

Beck nods, his expression set with resolution.

"Do you like tattooing?" he asks as I pull on my latex gloves and roll my stool forward.

"Yeah, I do. I hate it, though, when teenage girls and frat boys come in here wanting whatever popular bullshit is all the rage that week. Every time I have to ink a Chinese symbol or a quote from a popular movie, I die a little more inside."

Beck laughs and a warm sensation settles in my chest. *He has a really nice laugh.*

"What do you do?" I ask him.

"I'm a dancer."

The image of him in nothing but a lacy jock, wrapped around a stripper pole as he shakes his ass invades my brain and heats my skin before I shake it away.

"Uh, that's cool," I mutter, fixing my eyes on my work and forcing myself to focus.

We fall into an awkward silence.

I pay attention to Beck's physical reactions as I work. At first, he seems fine, but the longer I work, the more frequently I notice him tensing or holding his breath for a few seconds.

"I'm about finished with the outline. Do you mind if we finish up the color in a few weeks?" I offer, making it sound like it's for me rather than him.

"I didn't expect it to hurt this much, and I'm

worried if I don't finish now, I'll chicken out on coming back."

"Okay, we'll keep going then."

I put on some music to make my lack of desire to make small talk less noticeable and continue working on his ink.

By the time we're done, Beck is looking a little pale. But as soon as he looks at the vibrant peacock, a smile lights up his face.

"It's perfect. Oh my god, thank you so much. I can't tell you what this means," he gushes as I wipe off the excess ink and small blood droplets.

"You're welcome."

After bandaging his arm, I lead Beck up front to take payment and give him a print out of home care instructions. There's nothing worse than creating beautiful color work to see it fade and crack because it isn't properly cared for during healing.

"So, do you have a girlfriend...or boyfriend?" he asks when we reach the front desk.

I stop short, any warm, fluttery feelings I'd been experiencing earlier are suddenly slammed shut behind an impenetrable steel wall.

I grunt a non-committal response, then tell him the total he owes.

"Sorry, I'm sure it was wishful thinking on my part. I'm sure a guy like you is straight or already taken, or both."

Again, I don't respond, careful to keep my expression bland. The last thing I need is a sexy, endearing man interested in anything to do with me. I'm broken beyond repair. I'm shattered, and I can't be put back together.

"I hope I'll see you around," Beck says, lingering for a few seconds like he's hoping I'll suddenly thaw and return his sweet smile.

"Uh, sure, if you want some more ink, you know where to find me."

His face falls, but I can't miss the sway in his hips as he walks away.

Fortunately, I can't spend too much time dwelling on what a great ass he has because Nox is hovering near the desk.

"Hey, can we talk?"

I know this is about the way I acted last night when I caught Adam and Nox together. In my defense, I was caught off guard. I shouldn't have said the things I said to him. I know he feels guilty about Johnny's death. There's nothing Adam wouldn't have done for his brother, and I'm certain he's beat himself up over the same accusations I hurled at him last night. Adam being out or not wouldn't have made the difference in Johnny's decision to take his own life. If anyone is to blame, it's me. If anyone could have stopped Johnny from dying, it would've been me. I couldn't save him.

It's then I realize Nox is still waiting for a response from me.

"Sure," I agree.

"How about we go grab a drink after work and talk? I'll meet you over at O'Malley's?"

I nod before turning and heading back down the hall to my work area.

No matter which way I come at it, I can't wrap my mind around Adam being into guys. I thought we shared everything.

How many hours have I spent gutting myself open in front of him as I've mourned for Johnny? How many times when we were teenagers did we talk about people at school who we thought were hot? He could've told me. It would've been a simple statement to make.

I came out to him when we were sixteen for fuck's sake. He couldn't have told me then? Or literally any day in the thirteen years since?

And then to find out he's been secretly dating our roommate for months? What the fuck is that?

I can't decide which pain is gnawing harder in my gut; the betrayal or the crippling loneliness that comes with the realization that my best friend is in love with someone, and I'm going to lose him.

Then guilt rears up and joins the mix. There's no reason Adam shouldn't get to find someone to make him happy just because I'm too broken to ever love again.

I don't know why I agreed to talk to Nox before smoothing things out with Adam. I guess part of me wants to vet him like a best friend should. Is he good enough for Adam? It's a moot point now, seeing that they're already in love. But it feels like the right thing to do in the situation.

I stride down the street toward the bar, trying to decide what I'm going to say to Nox. Maybe I should call Adam and tell him to meet us.

I need to apologize to him. I need to pull my head out of my ass. I need to congratulate my best friend.

Now I'm thinking about it, Adam *has* been noticeably happier lately. I didn't entertain the idea he could be seeing someone because he never dated. Not serious dating anyway. He fucked around with girls like Kira, but he never showed any real interest.

As I near the bar, there's a weird shift in the air. I pause and glance around, trying to place the eerie feeling that has my hair standing on end.

The sound of scuffling comes from the alley beside the bar, so I creep closer to check if it's just a couple getting frisky or something more heinous.

What I see freezes my blood in my veins and kickstarts my heart.

Nox is limp with a strange man's arm around his throat. Nox's face is purple red as the man squeezes the life out of him.

I don't have time to stop and consider a course of action. I can't remember how long the brain can be deprived of oxygen before brain damage occurs, but I don't think it's long.

Without a second thought, I grab a large rock off the ground and lunge at the man.

He's too distracted to notice me so my blow lands hard and precise right to the back of his head.

The first impact is enough to get him to release his grip on Nox, whose body crumples to the ground.

I raise my arm and bring the rock down a second time just as the man is spinning around to face me, and I get him in the side of the head.

He goes down beside Nox.

I drop to my knees and check for a pulse on Nox before whipping out my phone.

"9-1-1, what is your emergency?"

"I need help. My friend was attacked outside of the bar, O'Malley's. Please hurry."

CHAPTER 2

Beck

I fly through the doors of On Point, the dance studio where I teach.

"Right on time, as always," my best friend, Clay, mocks.

I give him the finger as I jog down the hall to Studio One where I'm sure all my students are waiting, unsurprised that I'm late.

"Hey guys, sorry," I apologize as I hustle in. "I was getting a tattoo and I didn't realize how long it would take, then I needed to stop home and change," I explain, flailing my hands as I talk.

"Can we see your tattoo?" one of my favorite students, Kailee, asks.

Don't get me wrong, I love all the kids I teach. But at eight years old with an angel face, good behavior, and an astounding future ahead of her, I can't help but have a soft spot for her.

"Sure, it's a peacock," I explain as I slip my t-shirt off, leaving just my leotard on and my arms exposed.

One of the other girls giggles.

"Isn't that a bad word?"

I bite down hard on my bottom lip to keep

from laughing.

"No sweetie. It's a *pea*cock, which is a bird."

After all the kids have Oo'd and Ah'd over my new ink, I start shooing them all into place so we can get some work done before their parents show up to get them.

As I watch my kids dancing the moves I've taught them over the few months, my heart swells with pride while a familiar sadness courses through me simultaneously.

This has been my dream my entire life, to dance and foster the love of dance in kids. I just wish it hadn't taken the death of my twin sister Brianna to bring it about. And I wish I had the balls to tell my father to shove it so I could do this full time.

Once the class has ended and all the kids have been collected, Clay comes in to help me clean up.

"You finally got your tattoo," he notes with a smile. "How hard do you think your dad is going to flip out?"

"Ugh, don't remind me. It's not like he ever sees me in anything but a suit, so I think I can put off the fallout indefinitely."

"Good point," Clay agrees. "So, how was it?"

"Excruciating. Why didn't you tell me it would hurt so bad?" I complain. "It's still burning. How long until that goes away?"

Clay has two full sleeves of vibrant wild flowers; I can't imagine how long they took to complete.

"The burning will go away in a few hours. Except when you shower, it'll feel like a sunburn under water for a few days. Then the itching starts..." he explains, and I fix him with a look as the side effects pile up. "And it's so worth it, I didn't want you to chicken out."

I grumble a response. I *am* glad I got the peacock to remind me of Brianna.

"Where'd you go to get it done?"

"Heathens Ink, it's over by that bar you like, O'Malley's."

Clay's face lights up. He's a truly beautiful person inside and out, and when he smiles, it's enough to bring just about any man to his knees.

We fooled around a few times when we were teenagers, but ultimately decided we didn't feel anything but friendship for each other. Plus, it didn't take us long to realize we were both total bottoms. Not that I *never* top, but it has to be the right guy. As much as I love Clay, he's never been the right guy.

Clay and I met in my very first dance class when I was eight years old. My parents did everything they could to try to talk me out of taking a dance class. But I was at an age where I wanted to do whatever Brianna was doing, and she wanted to take ballet. They offered me every alternative under the sun from archery to horseback riding, money and time were no object. My heart was set on staying with my sister, though.

I didn't care when they told me no other boys would be there and that people might laugh at a boy for dancing ballet. I knew what I wanted, and I wouldn't be dissuaded.

They were wrong about there not being any other boys, but they weren't wrong about me being picked on over the years for dancing. Not that it was only the dancing I was picked on for. It was everything from the feminine way I gestured and moved, to the pretty clothes I liked to wear.

When we were teenagers, Clay asked me if I was transgender. I told him I didn't feel like a girl, I just liked the things they got to wear. And, frankly, I knew I looked fly as hell in makeup.

By the time we got to college, I realized it wasn't only frat boys and meatheads who had a problem with the way I dressed and acted. It turns out even gay men can be judgmental and cruel to each other.

I put all my silk and lace away in the back of my closet and threw my makeup away. I quit dance and focused all my energy on fitting in and getting through law school to please my parents.

Only two people saw how painful it was for me to bury the real Beck down so deep. Only two people saw the way I drank to mask the pain and let men use me so I'd feel valuable. Clay and Bri were the only ones who never lost sight of the real me, even when I wasn't sure who I was anymore.

"Oh my god, Heathens has the *hottest* tattoo artists," Clay swoons, pulling me out of my walk down memory lane.

The sexy, broody tattoo artist who worked on me today pops into my mind, and I feel a fresh wave of embarrassment. Ugh, what was wrong with me coming onto him like that when he wasn't giving me any indication he was interested? I mean, sure he was totally checking me out when I got there, but he was probably just trying to figure out what my deal was. Even if I had been dressed in my bro clothes today, I still had my makeup on.

"Yeah, the guy who did my ink had these intense eyes that made me stupid for a second. I asked him if he was seeing anyone; it was so embarrassing."

Clay snorts a laugh at me.

"Want to go grab a drink after I lock up?" Clay suggests.

"Can I take a rain check? I'm feeling kinda blah today."

"Of course, sweetie." Clay gives me a quick kiss on the cheek. "Do try to be on time tomorrow."

"Why put myself out when I've got my boss wrapped around my little finger?" I tease with a wink.

I flop down on my couch with a sigh.

Feeling lonely and a little sad tonight, I reach for my phone, bring up my Grindr app, and browse a little. It would be nice to get laid; it's been way too long.

As I swipe past profile after profile that declares 'no femmes' or 'masc. only', I let out an annoyed growl and toss my phone down.

"Ugh, Bri why'd you push me so hard to be myself. This shit sucks," I grumble at my empty apartment. So what if I still talk to my dead sister? My therapist said it was normal.

I head into the bathroom to wash my face and get comfortable for an exciting night in front of the TV alone.

I click on the music app on my phone and turn it to shuffle. When the first song is *Beautiful* by Christina Aguilera, I roll my eyes.

"Really, Bri, pulling out the Xtina to make your point? You're better than that." I push the little arrow to go to the next song. It's TLC's *Unpretty*, and I let out a long suffering sigh. "You're just as pushy now as you were when you were alive."

Another pang of loneliness hits me in the center of the chest.

I keep expecting the fractured feeling in my soul to get better, but it never seems to. I know Bri has only been gone for a year, but it would be great if I could stop reaching for my phone to text her.

CHAPTER 3

Gage

Standing in the hospital corridor with Officer Cas Bratton, I can't shake the image of Nox's face, purple from lack of oxygen. Or the way his body fell limp to the ground.

I don't know how long it took the ambulance to arrive, but it felt like an eternity. All I could think about was the gut wrenching pain of losing the person you love most in the world. I couldn't let that happen to Adam. No one should ever have to feel that.

It's difficult enough to get by day after day with only shards of a heart. But right now, I feel raw and exposed.

The scabs have been peeled away to reveal a wound still unhealed regardless of how many years have passed.

I'm back in that place again. I'm in the hospital with Johnny's family, with Adam, waiting to hear but already knowing.

No one ever tells you that about the death of a loved one. Somehow you just know. When Adam called me that night and said Johnny was being taken to the hospital, a heavy feeling settled in my gut, a voice in the back of my head telling me he was gone before I even knew what was wrong. It was as if I could sense his absence in the world the moment it happened.

Adam steps out of Nox's room, a sense of exhausted relief oozing from every pore. Without preamble, he marches up to me and wraps his arms around me in a fierce hug.

"You saved his life. I'll never be able to thank you enough. I don't know what I would've done..."

"Of course I helped him. I don't need you to thank me."

"I'm sorry for lying to you. I've been carrying around guilt over this for so many years. It spiraled. Every day I didn't tell you the truth, it got harder. I never meant to hurt you." Adam's voice falters at the end, and I hug him tighter.

Yes, I was angry, and yes, I was hurt. But none of that matters now.

"I know, and I shouldn't have said what I did. It was out of line, and I didn't believe it for an instant. I was hurt, and I lashed out. Never for a second have I ever thought you bore any responsibility for Johnny's death." *Because I'm responsible for Johnny's death. If I'd been a better boyfriend, more observant, if I'd only known...*I pat his back. "Let's forget about it. I love you man. I want you to be happy, and I'm glad you found a guy who's right for you."

"Thank you."

"I guess I'd better start looking for a new place to live, huh?" I muse as I pull back from the hug.

Another wave of loneliness washes over me. This was bound to happen eventually. Of course, Adam wasn't going to be single forever. In the back of my mind I knew one day I'd have to give up the comfort of his presence, the dependence on him to support me and keep me grounded.

The thought of an apartment all to myself is enough to steal my breath and ice my veins. The apartment I'd always pictured sharing with Johnny will be an empty one instead. No one to come home to at the end of the night. No one to sit up with when I can't sleep.

But I can't hold on to Adam forever. He deserves his happiness, no matter what it might cost me.

"What? Why?" Adam asks.

"You and Nox are all couple-y now. You don't need me cramping your style. It's past time anyway. I've been leaning on you way too long. You deserve to have a life that doesn't revolve around your mopey best friend."

"My life will *always* revolve around my mopey best friend," Adam jokes.

I force what I'm sure is an unconvincing smile.

"Nah, you've got your man now. Go be happy. I'll still be here, I'll just be trying to prop myself up for a change."

"I'll be here for you, no matter what. That won't ever change."

"Thanks, man."

"Hey, would you mind if I borrow your car tonight?" I ask.

"Of course. I'm staying here with Nox, so it's yours. You'll just have to Uber home to get it since I rode in with Cas."

"Guess a car is another thing I'll need if I'm getting my own place," I muse.

"Might be nice to have your own car," Adam points out, and I nod in agreement.

I give Adam one last hug before ordering an Uber and going outside to wait.

I feel like my skin is too tight, and my insides are too sharp. I'm coming apart at the seams.

As soon as I pull into the familiar spot at the hidden overlook, I'm assaulted with so many memories it's almost impossible to breathe.

Flashes of images pass before my eyes like still shots from a familiar movie. Johnny smiling at me with so much shy hope, I laid my heart at his feet that very moment. His small frame in my arms as we lay breathless and tangled on a blanket, sweat cooling on our skin, gazing up at the stars and dreaming of a future. Tears and fights because he couldn't stand keeping our love a secret, while I tried for the millionth time to explain to him why it wasn't the right time to tell Adam. Johnny growing increasingly more distant as I begged literally on hands and knees for him to tell me what was going on with him, desperate to know why he wasn't the same man I fell in love with anymore. Where was *my* Johnny, and who was that shell of a boy in his place?

I should've seen the signs then. I should've known that he needed more help than the sheer strength my love alone could give him.

And then, the night Adam and I drove up here after Johnny's funeral and drowned our sorrows in a bottle of Jack.

The force of the memories nearly brings me to my knees. I haven't come up here since that night with Adam. I couldn't bear it. It's too much of Johnny and not enough all at the same time.

I'm a husk of a person now. I'm a man without a heart or soul. When Johnny died, he took those things with him and left a painful ache where they used to be.

I sink down on the ground beside Adam's car and look up at the night sky. It looks the same as it always did when Johnny was in my arms. How can the universe be so unaffected by the loss of such a beautiful soul? How can life continue to go on day after day without him?

"How could you do this to me Jay? You promised me forever. I know we were young, but I believed you. Everyone says things get better with time, so why does it feel so fucking raw still? Why do I still wake up thinking for a second you're still here? Why can't I move on? It's been nine years Jay. Why can't I get the fuck over it? And why did you have to leave me? Why?" My voice cracks as the tears roll freely down my cheeks. "I can't keep living like this Jay. When I promised it would only ever be you, I meant it from the bottom of my heart. But you're gone now, and I'm so lonely I can't breathe. I can't do it anymore. I can't."

A broken sob escapes my chest, and I bury my face in my hands.

At least no one is up here to see me breaking down like this.

I know what they all think of me. They can't understand how I can still be mourning the loss of someone who died almost a decade ago. But Johnny wasn't *someone;* he was *everything.* He was my first and only love.

I can still remember the night we got together like it was yesterday. I still dream of it.

I had known Johnny his whole life, and he had always been my best friend's goofy little brother. Kind of cute and so campy you'd think he was *trying* to be every gay stereotype he could manage. But that was just Johnny. He didn't care what people thought. At least, I didn't think he cared. Maybe if I'd realized how much it really mattered to him he'd still be here now.

He was sixteen, and I was twenty, and I felt like

31

a skeeve for noticing how hot he was. It wasn't just a physical attraction, though. It was like I couldn't get enough of his company. I kept finding excuses to hang out with him so I could absorb some of his happy glow.

He'd had a hard day at school, and he'd come home visibly upset, almost in tears. No one was around, so I did something I'd never done before, something I'd been craving to do. I put my arms around him and held him against my chest.

"What can I do to make it better, Jay? Tell me, I'll do anything," I'd asked, tilting his head up so I could brush his tears away with my thumbs.

He looked up at me through his eyelashes, with the most serious expression I'd ever seen on his normally smiling face.

"You can stop pretending there's nothing between us and kiss me already."

I gasped at his bold statement.

"Jay...I..."

He didn't wait for me to think of a million reasons it would be wrong for us to kiss. Instead, he reared up on his toes and pressed his soft lips to mine.

My entire world shattered in that moment and reformed with Johnny at the center of it. There was never any choice for me other than loving Johnny.

"You have to let me go, Jay. Please, let me go."

A warm breeze wraps around me, and I could almost swear I can smell Johnny's favorite cologne for a millisecond. And for the first time in so many years, a small amount of peace settles over my heart. It's almost as if Johnny heard my plea and is trying to tell me it's okay to move on.

"I'll always love you, Jay. No matter what else ever happens in my life, you will always be the biggest piece of my heart."

CHAPTER 4

Two Months Later

Gage

"What are you doing tonight?" Adam asks after I settle with my last client for the day.

"No plans." I shrug.

"You're coming out with us, then. We're going to this all male dancing and burlesque thing. It's going to be a blast."

"It's still so weird to me to think of you being into guys," I muse.

"If you need verification of how much I love getting fucked by a man, Nox can vouch for me," he teases.

I cringe at the image of my best friend having sex with *anyone*.

"Gross, dude."

Adam slugs me in the arm and laughs.

"You're coming, right?"

"I guess," I agree half-heartedly. I can't think of an excuse not to, so it'll be easier to do it rather than argue.

"Try not to sound so enthusiastic."

"Wouldn't dream of it."

"How'd you hear about this, anyway?" I ask Adam when we're all seated in a crowded theater downtown.

"It's the weirdest thing; I got an invite to this event from Johnny's memorial Facebook account. Must've been some kind of glitch. Isn't that creepy?"

"That's kind of fucked up."

"Yeah," Adam agrees with a shrug. "Seemed cool though, so I'm not going to skip it just because of an unsettling glitch. This'll be fun; try to enjoy it."

I nod in agreement and settle back in my seat as the house lights flicker in warning that the show's about to start.

I have to admit these guys are talented. One performance after another comes and goes from the stage, varying from classic burlesque dancers to what seem to be modern dance troupes. All of them are astounding in their talent. When the second to last group of dancers take the stage, my breath catches when I recognize Beck, the guy I tattooed two months ago.

Beck, along with seven other guys, is standing in two lines on the stage. They're all wearing red high heels and black body suits. The music starts out slow, and their movements match it, mesmerizing and fluid. Then it transitions to a faster hip-hop beat, and they bust out some complicated and awe-inspiring dance moves. My eyes are trained on Beck the entire time. The way his body rolls and flits along to the beat has me unable to tear my attention away.

His face is a mask of ecstasy as his being becomes music personified. Breathtaking is the only word I can come up with for it.

I'm still in a daze when he leaves the stage, and I don't even see the next performance because my mind is too busy replaying everything about Beck.

When the lights come back on, and everyone starts to shuffle toward the exits, it still takes me a few minutes to shake my brain out of the fog.

"Let's grab a drink at Miller's," Adam suggests, pointing at a bar a few buildings down.

Everyone agrees, and as I shove my hands into my pockets, I realize I don't have my phone.

"Shit, I think my phone fell out of my pocket. I'll meet you guys over there; I need to go back in."

Beck

On the darkened stage in the empty theater, I go over the place in the dance again where I hadn't felt totally natural. I manage the step with a little more confidence this time so I go for it again just to be sure.

After my fourth time, I look up and notice

the tattoo artist guy with the pink hair standing in the otherwise abandoned theater watching me.

"Hey," I call out, giving him an acknowledging head tilt.

"Hey," he says in return. "Sorry, I dropped my phone, and when I came back you were dancing..."

"It's okay. This might come as a shock but I don't mind people watching me dance."

"You're really good. How'd you get into this? Is it a hobby or a full-time thing?"

A lump fills the back of my throat, and my legs feel weak. It's impossible to answer that question truthfully without talking about Brianna. But for some reason I *want* to tell him.

"I've always loved dancing, and when I was young, I dreamed of it as a career. But, you know how life tends to happen. I woke up one day in a career I hate and no time to enjoy anything, let alone time for dancing. Then, a year ago, my twin sister died." I swallow, trying to moisten my mouth. "She was fine, thirty and healthy. Then one day, BAM, brain aneurysm. The doctor said there was no way she could've known her head was a ticking time bomb. It made me realize how short life is, and that I needed to *make* time to enjoy things." I open my hands to gesture to the theater around us. "Bri would've been proud; she was always pushing me to pursue passions instead of wasting away behind a desk. I'm still waiting for that time heals all wounds thing to kick in."

"It doesn't," Gage jumps in, his tone soft and sad. "Eventually it'll get softer around the edges. But that person's missing presence will always be there."

"Who was it for you?"

His face falls, and I can tell he's struggling with the words. When he looks back up at me, his eyes are shining with pain.

"My boyfriend, Johnny. It was almost ten years ago."

"I'm sorry for your loss."

"Thanks. I'm sorry for yours, too."

"Is it just me or does a depressing conversation like this call for a drink?"

"Oh, well, I'm supposed to meet my friends at Miller's, down the street."

"Good. I bet they even have drinks there. You can buy me one." I wink at him before hopping down off the stage. "Mind waiting two minutes for me to get changed?"

Gage looks surprised but nods in agreement.

I strut back toward the changing room, adding a little extra swing to my hips. Gage is cute, and I'm a sucker for the whole wounded soul thing. Plus, he said *boyfriend*, which means I have a chance.

In the dressing room, I change out of my costume and slip into a pair of leggings and a purple, off the shoulder shirt. It's very *Flashdance*. Then, I trade my heels for ballet flats and touch up my makeup. Giving myself a quick once-over in the mirror, I declare myself ready for my impromptu sort of date with hottie tattoo artist.

When I step back out into the auditorium, I'm half surprised to find Gage waiting. I pegged him at even odds as a flight risk.

His eyes roam over me, and when they land on my feet, there's no mistaking the disappointment.

"I know, the heels make my legs and ass look phenomenal. They kill my feet though, so I needed a break from them after dancing. If you play your cards right, I might be persuaded to wear them special just for you sometime."

Gage's face flames bright red, and his eyes go wide.

He's going to be a fun challenge, I can already tell.

Gage

The image fills my mind of Beck with his toned legs around my waist, high heels biting into the back of my thighs as I pound into him.

A hot pool of lust settles in the pit of my stomach, leaving me breathless.

I haven't felt this way since Johnny died. Not that I've been celibate for eight years. But, this feeling of all-consuming *need* is something I didn't think I was capable of anymore.

Guilt is hot on the heels of the lustful surge.

I promised Johnny he'd be the only one for me until the day I die. I never considered the horrible possibility that he'd be gone, and I'd still be here.

When we get to the bar, I spot the guys taking over a few tables in the far corner. They all look so happy these days. Each of them touching, kissing, or staring longingly at their boyfriends.

I'm happy for them, but being the odd man out isn't a great time.

"Only single guy in the group?" Beck notes, following my gaze.

"Owen is single." I point at the only one of my friends who isn't in a relationship. He looks perfectly content, though, not painfully lonely like I am. "But otherwise, yeah."

"That sucks."

I shrug. It *does* suck, but I never expected my friends to be lonely, miserable bastards the rest of their lives like me.

"What are you drinking?" I ask, turning toward the bar top.

"Whatever's on tap. I'm not picky."

My surprise must show on my face because Beck cocks his hip and glares at me.

"You thought I was going to want some high-maintenance drink, didn't you?" he accuses.

Rather than incriminate myself, I ignore the question, flag down the bartender, and order two of whatever's on tap. Once we're equipped with drinks, Beck turns to me and gives me a sweet smile.

"I can be your boo for the night if you want," he offers and then flutters his impossibly long eyelashes at me.

"My boo?"

"Yeah, you know, your man, your sugar lips, your love bug..."

"Okay, I get it." I put my hands up as if to ward off all the cutesy nicknames he's suggesting.

"Just trying to be helpful."

"I appreciate it, but if I walk over there with a boo, they'd have to assume an Invasion of the Body Snatchers scenario."

"You don't date much?"

"Try ever," I correct.

Beck takes a sip of his beer, and I'm amazed to see he doesn't leave so much as a smudge of red lipstick on the rim of the glass. I wonder if it rubs off during a prolonged make out session, or if he's ever left a cock smeared with his lip color.

"What about sex?"

I sputter and choke on the drink I just took.

"What about sex?"

"Do you have any?" Beck asks in a conversational tone.

"That's forward, especially since we don't know each other."

Beck shrugs.

"Didn't realize you were a prude."

"I'm *not* a prude. I just don't want to discuss my sex life with a stranger," I snap.

"You're feisty; I like it."

I let out an irritated huff. I should've bolted while he was getting changed. I must be out of my mind.

"Come on before I change my mind." I jerk my head in the direction of my friends, and Beck follows.

As soon as we near the tables, I feel seven sets of eyes boring into me, expressions ranging from concerned to gleefully curious.

Except for Adam, none of them have ever seen me with a man before. Not that I'm *with* Beck.

"My, my, who do we have here?" Royal asks.

"I'm Beck," he introduces himself.

"Nice to meet you Beck," Royal says. The shimmer in his eye tells me I'm going to get shit for this later. "These are my boyfriends Nash and Zade. Over there is Madden and his fiancé, Thane. Adam and his boyfriend Nox are on the end. And the gorgeous single guy is Owen." Royal points to each person in turn, and Beck tries to follow.

"How do you know Gage?" Adam asks.

"He tattooed me a couple months ago. I bumped into him as I was leaving the theater just now after the show. He practically begged me to come out with him," Beck exaggerates. "I think he's trying to get in my pants," he stage-whispers, and Royal nearly spits his drink out.

"I like this guy," Madden announces, scooting his chair over to make room for Beck.

I'm not surprised that in about thirty seconds flat Beck fits right into my group of friends like he's been here all along. I get the feeling he's simply that kind of person. The type who makes friends everywhere he goes, never feeling like the odd man out.

The pain I saw in his eyes when we were at the theater when he mentioned his sister is gone now, but I can't say the smile on his lips entirely reaches his eyes either.

I hear the quiet murmur of Adam's voice as he whispers something to Nox who then laughs. I get the distinct impression that they're talking about me, but I ignore them. It's not until Beck looks over at me in the middle of a conversation he's having with Madden and winks at me that I realize I've been staring at him.

My eyes drop to my drink, and I become extremely fascinated with the carbonation bubbles in my glass.

Beck's elbow jabs into my ribs and then the heat of his body envelopes me as he leans close and whispers.

"Is it bothering you for me to be here? I can go if it is."

"No," I say too quickly. I don't understand why, but I like having Beck here. Even though I don't know him. "Stay. I'm just like...*this*. I feel like I'm going through life in a fog most of the time. It's nice having you here; you're full of color."

Beck bats his eyelashes at me.

"If I didn't know any better, I'd think you *like* me, Gage."

"I don't know you," I point out to deflect the accusation. The truth is, I can't remember what it's like to feel much of anything, let alone *like* or lust.

"You know something no one else knows."

"About your sister?"

Beck nods, his face solemn for a second.

"What would you need to know to decide if you like me?" he teases.

"Uh..."

"All right, well I'm Beck, as you already know, I'm thirty-one, and I have a serious obsession with starburst and looking fly as hell. I also love sleeping in on weekends and watching sappy rom coms. Yes, I am a stereotype in that sense, no shame. I have a cat who's a total asshole, but he belonged to Bri so I'm stuck with him, but I'd much rather have a dog eventually. Let's see..." He taps his chin as he thinks. "My first kiss was in the eighth grade, and it was really nasty because it was just after lunch, and he had major pizza breath."

"Okay, I officially know everything about you." I hold up my hands in defense.

"Not everything, sugar. I was just getting to my favorite sex position."

"Jesus Christ," I mutter and take a deep gulp of my beer. This guy is too much.

"Nope, just Beck," he jokes.

"You still riding back with us?" Adam asks me, his eyes flicking between Beck and myself.

I almost wish I'd driven my own car tonight, but Adam had been convinced if he didn't pick me up I would've flaked. He was probably right.

"Yeah, of course."

I stand up and turn toward Beck, wondering how to say goodbye to someone I don't know.

Without warning, Beck reaches into my pocket and retrieves my phone. Before I can protest, he's tapping away and then handing it back seconds later.

"Text me some time," Beck suggests with a wink. "And by the way, it's sixty-nine," he calls over his shoulder as he sashays away.

"Damn, check out your game, scoring that cutie's digits without even trying," Royal ribs me.

"I wasn't...What do I even do with his number?" I ask, staring at my phone like it's a bomb.

"Call him?" Madden suggests.

My gut clenches at the thought.

"I *can't.*"

Part of me wants to call. Part of me is dying to find out more about the intriguing, beautiful man with an inexplicable interest in me. But I'm not sure I'm ready, or if I'll ever be.

Adam's hand lands on my shoulder, and he gives it a squeeze.

"You know Johnny would've wanted you to be happy, don't you? He would have never wanted to see you this lonely."

I shrug off his touch, my blood starting to boil.

"We'll never know what Johnny would've wanted."

"Exactly," Adam presses, refusing to back down and getting my hackles up even further.

"I can't deal with this. I'm going to walk for a bit and then get an Uber." I spin and head out of the bar before anyone can try to stop me. My heart is spasming in my chest, and my lungs feel tight. No one can tell me how Johnny would've wanted me to deal with this. Anyway, it doesn't matter what Johnny would've wanted; he's gone, and I'm here. Fucking alone.

CHAPTER 5

Beck

"The usual, honey?"

"You know it," I smile up at Trisha, the waitress who's been serving Clay and me during our weekly Sunday breakfast for the past year. "Clay will be here any minute."

"Of course."

Right on cue, Clay hurries in looking like he's still half-asleep.

"Long night?" I guess as I slide the carafe of coffee toward him.

"Yeah, but not in a fun way."

"Bummer. Your date didn't go well?" I ask.

Clay had been looking forward to this date all week, and I think I was hoping as hard as he was that things would go well. As attractive and wonderful as Clay is, he has the damndest time making it past a first date. I don't know if he's just inordinately picky or if there's something else getting in the way. I have yet to find a tactful way to ask.

"Total bust. I ended up at home with Max watching *Pitch Perfect* for the hundredth time."

The gooey smile he tries to hide when he mentions his roommate Max makes me think that might be the crux of his dating problem. Sadly, Max is straight, at least in theory.

"Enough about my pathetic love life. I saw you leaving the theater with a hottie after the show the other night; what was up with that?"

My stomach flutters at the mention of Gage, and I'm sure my own goofy grin gives away the little crush I'm developing on Mr. Broody-And-Tattooed.

"Yeah, he's the tattoo artist from Heathens who did my ink a few months ago. He was at the show that night, and we ran into each other. I ended up grabbing a drink with him and his friends," I explain in as casual a tone as I can muster.

"Is he...nice?" Clay asks carefully, taking a sip of his coffee, his eyes remaining trained on me over his mug.

"So far," I shrug. Truth is, sometimes it's hard to tell at first. I've had guys seem perfectly cool with my makeup and clothes and then flip the script out of nowhere and start acting like I'm some sort of freak. Or worse, treat me like I'm nothing more than a kinky fuck before ghosting.

"You've gotta give me more than that," Clay complains.

"He's a wounded soul," I confide.

"Mmm, just your type," Clay laughs.

"Is it so wrong of me to want to hug and kiss them all better?" I feign offense. "Seriously though, he seems really sweet, but I'm not sure he's interested in what I'm selling. I gave him my number, so we'll see."

Clay seems convinced enough about my nonchalance regarding whether or not I'll see Gage again. What I didn't tell Clay is that I've been checking my phone obsessively for the past two days, hoping for a text or call. Not just because Gage is hot and just my type, but because something inside me was soothed by being in the presence of someone who might be able to understand my pain.

Gage

I've never lived alone. I went from living with my parents to rooming with Adam and never looked back. I underestimated just how quiet an apartment can be. Not that Adam was a particularly noisy roommate, but it's almost like his presence generated white noise.

Adam and Nox told me repeatedly there was no need for me to move out, but it was something I had to do for myself as much as for them. The last thing a new couple needs is a depressing roommate. The happiness and love radiating from them was too much to bear on a constant basis.

I turn on the TV and settle back, not really interested in watching anything but needing the background noise to fill my too quiet apartment.

A sense of restlessness settles over me, and for some reason, I have the overwhelming urge to text Beck. But what would be the point? There's one reason a guy gives you his number: he's looking for a hook-up. Granted, it's been ages since I've gotten laid, and Beck is undoubtedly my type, but something about it seems wrong. Beck seems cool; I wouldn't want to use him and drop him. And something about him is too warm and enticing; it's too much.

I'm not sure why I want to text him anyway, if not for a booty call.

I let out a frustrated huff at myself and sit up slightly to fluff the cushion behind me on the couch, determined to relax and get comfortable.

My phone vibrates, and I nearly drop it in surprise. For a second, my heart leaps at the idea it might be Beck calling, until I realize I never gave him my number.

I glance down at it and see it's Adam calling.

"Hey, man," I answer.

"Hey, thought you might want to go grab a drink? It's been a minute since we've had any time to shoot the shit or whatever."

"That's because you've been busy with your tongue down your man's throat," I tease.

"That's not the only place my tongue has been."

"Dude, gross. I don't need to have any mental images of what you and Nox get up to in bed."

"Yeah, yeah," Adam chuckles. "So, drink?"

"Yeah, I'll meet you down at O'Malley's in twenty."

By the time I get there, Adam is already sitting at the bar, nursing a beer. There's also a second beer in the open seat beside him. Sliding into the empty seat, I give him a nod of thanks as I lift the beer to my lips.

"So, how's your new place?" Adam asks.

I shrug and focus on the ring of condensation from my drink left on the wood so I don't look at Adam and give myself away.

"It's fine."

"Is it?" He doesn't sound convinced. "Because I miss my best friend like crazy."

I put my hand on Adam's shoulder and give it a grateful squeeze, still avoiding eye contact; this time because I'm worried I might get sappy if I look at him.

"Come on man, I'm sure you're too busy with Nox to even notice I'm gone. I'm not stupid; I know what it's like to be in love." My heart gives a sad squeeze. I didn't have Johnny for long, but fuck if I didn't love him with every inch of my being.

"That doesn't mean I don't miss hanging out with you. We've been joined at the hip our entire lives. I do love Nox, more than anything, but that doesn't mean I don't miss our late-night Netflix marathons and those god-awful smoothies you make."

"Those are really good for you," I argue with

a laugh. "You should try those instead of donuts and shit for breakfast."

"I prefer a protein shake these days." Adam waggles his eyebrows, and I groan.

"Well, I miss you too. But, I still think this was the right move. You and Nox need your space and I need..." *What do I need?* A re-do? A memory wipe? A way to move on.

"To get laid?" Adam suggests. I make a non-committal noise and take another gulp of my drink. "And on that topic, are you going to call Beck?"

I run my hand through my hair and then start to peel away the label on my beer bottle while forcing my brain not to even contemplate Adam's question or it's implication.

"Y'all need anything?" Beau, the sexy bartender, asks, buying me a few seconds to figure out how to respond to Adam's question.

"No thanks, Beau."

"Hey, how's Cas been? I haven't seen him down here recently," Adam asks. Cas Bratton, the cop who tried to help Nox when he was being stalked by his ex, also happens to be Beau's roommate.

The little smile on Beau's face at the mention of Cas makes it clear how much Cas means to him.

"He's been busy at work. He's working for a promotion to detective, so it's been crazy."

"That's awesome; he deserves it."

"Thanks, I'll tell him you said hi."

"So, are you going to call Beck?" Adam asks again, and I let out a huff of a breath.

"Probably not."

"Why?" Adam presses.

"What would be the point?" I challenge.

"The *point?*" Adam's tone is dripping with disbelief and frustration. "You know what? Let's drop this subject because it's clearly not going anywhere productive."

"Thank you."

"Don't mention it," Adam says sarcastically before putting an arm over my shoulder and giving me an awkward side hug. "So, let's talk about fundraising for Rainbow House instead, that seems like a safe subject."

I let out a relieved breath and finally turn to face my best friend.

"I love the idea of giving them a percentage of the profits from Heathens on certain days that Nox came up with. The question is how do we market it to bring people in?"

CHAPTER 6

Beck

"Just call him already," Clay suggests with a hint of exasperation in his voice.

I use one hand to flip my phone over so I can't keep peeking at the screen as I hold the downward dog position I'm in. I glance over to give Clay an apologetic smile and chuckle at the ease with which he's twisted himself into a pretzel.

"How are you single?"

"Sweetie, that is not a can of worms you want to open. Now stop deflecting. Why haven't you called him? It's been two weeks, right?"

"Two and a half weeks," I grumble. "I can't call him because my dumb ass didn't get his number."

"So, what? You know where he works; go down there."

"Isn't that too pushy?"

Clay snorts a laugh at my comment as I move into Warrior pose.

"Since when are you concerned about being too pushy with a guy?"

"Fair point," I concede.

"You've been checking your phone constantly since you gave him your number. I'm just saying you should either go get him or get over it."

I consider Clay's words as I move into Sun pose. I *have* been obsessively waiting to hear from Gage, even long past the length of time when I usually give up on holding my breath that a guy will call. Maybe it's because after he told me about his boyfriend, things snapped into place, and I could understand why he wasn't all that receptive to my flirting. Or maybe it's just because there is something about him that makes me feel like I *need* to know more about him.

A few hours later I'm alone in my apartment once again, sitting on the opposite end of the couch from Frodo and absentmindedly browsing Grindr.

I pause on a decently cute guy with blue hair, but my mind immediately goes to Gage's pink hair. It seems so out of place for him. There must be a story there, and for some reason I'm dying to know what it is.

I swipe left to reject him and sigh in exasperation.

Clay was right; I either need to go down to Heathens or get over it. I'm not a guy who pines. Even when my douchey ex took off, I didn't pine.

I might have moped for a week, but then I moved the fuck on. I sure as shit never sat around waiting for my phone to ring.

Gage

I pace my apartment like a caged lion, looking for any sort of distraction. I almost wish I had a drug habit like Madden and Nox just to have some damn thing to take the edge off this unbearable feeling of something crawling under my skin. It's like there's an energy inside me desperate to burst out but with nowhere to go.

For the first several years after Johnny died, I was lucky to have enough energy to get through the day. Some days I couldn't even manage to get out of bed. The loneliness was a physical presence weighing me down. And at least in my dreams or half-awake stupor, I could forget Johnny was gone.

But somewhere along the way, roughly three years ago, I started having moments where I wanted to scream and thrash, anything to release everything pent up inside. It's like I was desperate for something I couldn't put my finger on.

Two years ago, I thought I'd try fucking it out. Seemed like as good an idea as any. Fucking made it worse. Touching a man I didn't know made me almost physically ill and made the storm inside me rage harder.

This wasn't how it was supposed to be. I'm not supposed to have an empty bed and a broken heart.

I look at my phone for the umpteenth time since I ran into Beck.

Why would he even want someone like me to text him? For a hook-up? That seems like the most likely reason. It's not like I have anything to offer him. And I can't offer him a hook-up either. Well...maybe I could, but what would be the point?

I run my thumb absentmindedly along the rounded corners of my phone, simultaneously wishing for strength and a moment of sanity.

"Tell you what, Jay, if this is the right thing, then give me a sign. Show me it's time for me to move on."

I'm sitting at the front desk at Heathens, uploading a few images to our Facebook page when a familiar voice breaks my thoughts.

"He lives."

I whip my head around and, sure enough, standing not five feet away is the man I haven't been able to stop thinking about for two weeks.

"What?" I ask, trying to understand the meaning of his seemingly incomplete sentence.

"You're alive, and you don't seem to have a head injury or any sort of damage to your hands that would prevent you from using your phone."

"Uh, no?"

"What gives, then?" Beck demands, hands

on his hips. "I gave you my number, and you never called or texted."

I feel the heat rising in my cheeks.

"I...um...uh..."

"Maybe you *do* have a head injury," Beck grumbles, moving his hands from his hips to cross over his chest, accusing gaze fixed on me.

"I didn't want a *hook-up*," I whisper the last word and glance around to make sure no one heard me.

Beck purses his lips like he's trying not to laugh at me.

"Oh, relax honey, I'm not going to blowjob rape you."

I sputter, trying to come up with something to say in return, and I come up blank.

After a few seconds, Beck's gaze softens, and he leans over the desk. My eyes are fixated on his luscious deep red lips.

"I was kind of hoping we could be friends," Beck says, his tone much gentler now.

"Why?"

"We're both broken, and it seems like our jagged edges might fit together well. I think it would be nice to hang out with someone who understands the pain without looking at me with pity."

His words resound in my heart.

"Yeah, that seems okay, I guess."

"You're a real sweet talker, aren't you?" Beck winks at me before pushing off the desk. "What are you doing tonight after work?"

"Nothing."

"You are now. Come by my place, I'll order take-out, and we can chill," he suggests. I open my mouth to clarify, but Beck puts a hand over my mouth before I can speak. "*Not* Netflix and Chill. Regular chill with all our clothes on and no one getting their rocks off. Boring chill."

"Sounds good."

Beck leans over the desk once more, this time grabbing a scrap of paper and a pen off the employee side. He jots something down and passes it to me.

"Here's my address. You already know now I *will* hunt you down if you stand me up. I'll see you later."

"Later," I agree, in a slight daze as Beck practically prances out of the shop.

I shift on my feet and raise my fist to knock on Beck's door. It's the third time I've attempted a knock only to pull back at the last second. I can't figure out what I'm doing here or whether I hope Beck was lying or telling the truth about not wanting to hook-up.

I rap quickly against the door before I lose my nerve again, and a split second later, the door flies open.

"I was wondering how many false starts you were going to have. I made a bet with myself it would be more than five."

"It was only three; what do you lose?"

"If I won, I'd have let myself think about you when I jerk off later."

I pull up short, my mouth falling open and the tips of my ears burning.

"I'm just teasing you, sugar. Come on in."

I'm still floundering for something to say as I step into his apartment.

"Listen, I know I suggested chilling here, but I'm feeling all—" Beck flails his arms around to demonstrate his emotions. "Do you mind if we go grab a beer or something and maybe play pool?"

"Yeah, that sounds good."

Beck's shoulders sag in relief.

"Okay, let me just go throw on some shoes really quick."

As he turns to head down the hallway off his living room, I finally get my bearings enough to glance around. My first thought is that this place is so *Beck*.

There's a warm sort of chaos in the room, everything seeming to be just slightly out of place. The walls are decorated with posters that seem to be French advertisements. Near the door there are several pairs of what I can only guess to be dance shoes. I recognize ballet shoes, but the rest are a mystery to me. On the couch there's a grumpy looking cat, perched on a blue throw blanket, glaring at me.

"Don't mind Frodo; he's an asshole," Beck says, gesturing at the cat when he comes back into the room.

"Your sister's cat, right?"

"Yeah, he was only nice to Bri. I took him in, and how does he repay me? He pisses in my bed, eats my shoes, and god help me if I try to do yoga in the living room." Beck shudders for emphasis.

"Poor guy, I bet he misses her," I coo as I stoop down to appear less threatening to the fluffy squish face who's still looking at me like he's plotting to piss on something I own.

"Yeah, I think he does," Beck agrees in a more subdued tone. "That blanket was Bri's; Frodo hardly ever leaves it."

When I finally tear my gaze away from the cat, I see Beck; my heart stutters, and my skin heats.

He's dressed in a pink, gauzy top that I'm sure would be soft to the touch. Paired with the top is a pair of black shorts, showing off miles of toned, smooth legs. And on his feet, are a pair of pink high heels. My dick shifts as it fills. I never thought a man in heels could be so fucking hot, but goddamn, if it doesn't work for Beck.

When I notice his toes are painted with shimmery silver polish, a smile twists on my lips. I don't know why but there's something so sweet and pretty about it.

"Is there a problem?" Beck asks with a defensive edge in his voice.

I wrench my attention away from his sparkly toes and look at his face. I don't see the irritation that was etched in his tone. Instead, I see apprehension.

"No problem. I...like your shoes."

Beck narrows his eyes at me in suspicion.

"Are you getting weird about going out in public with a guy wearing *women's* shoes?" he challenges.

"Not at all, but if I beat you at pool, you'd better not blame the shoes." I wink at him and find myself surprised by my teasing tone. Am I flirting?

Beck's expression morphs from tentative to cocky.

"You're underestimating me, sugar."

Beck

I hide my sigh of relief as Gage and I head out of my apartment without further discussion on the topic of my clothing.

"There's a great little pub right down the street." I wave Gage in the right direction.

A comfortable silence falls between us as we walk, the quiet night only punctuated by the clicking of my heels.

"Are those comfortable?" Gage asks.

My body tenses, ready to defend my choices. But when I glance at Gage, I don't see any hint of judgment in his face. He looks curious.

"Not particularly, but they look fantastic.

And as my mother used to say, 'beauty is pain'," I laugh.

The bar is dead, which isn't surprising for a Wednesday night.

"Hey beautiful, nice shoes," Tony, the bartender, calls when he spots me.

"Are you trying to get me in bed, love?" I accuse playfully.

"Always."

Gage grunts beside me, and when I look over, I see his jaw set in a hard line. If I didn't know any better, I'd think he's feeling a little jealous.

"Beer, right?"

Gage nods.

"Two beers, Tony," I shout and then drag Gage over to the pool table.

"Are you dating that guy?"

"Tony? God no," I laugh. "He's straight. He's just a flirt and I tip well." I shrug.

The tension in his shoulders relaxes. Gage grabs some pool cues while I rack the balls.

"Tell me about dancing," Gage prompts.

"What do you want to know?"

"How'd you get into it?"

"I took my first dance class when I was eight because I absolutely *had* to do everything Bri did. The thing was, she wanted to quit after the first month, but I had already fallen in love with it. My parents were *pissed*." I laugh, remembering the way my dad's head nearly exploded when I insisted on staying in dance after Bri quit.

"Why did Bri want to quit?" Gage asks as he bends over to take his first shot. He's asking so casually, but it's like he sees into my heart and knows how much it would mean to me to have a chance to talk about Bri in a happy way rather than thinking about the pain.

"She was such a perfectionist. She never wanted to do anything unless she was, like, a prodigy at it right away."

Gage laughs.

"What did she do for work?"

"Stripper."

Surprise flashes across his face and then uncertainty.

"Seriously?"

"No," I chuckle. "She was a Kindergarten teacher."

Tony brings our beer over, and I give him a generous tip, as always.

"Is there anything you want to tell me about your boyfriend?" I ask Gage gently, wanting him to know I'm happy to listen to him too if he wants to talk about it.

"Johnny." Gage supplies his name. "Uh…" He clears his throat and looks down at his feet, and when he looks up at me again I notice a slight glassy sheen to his eyes.

"We don't have to talk about him," I backpedal.

"No, we can. Sorry, it's just that no one mentions him to me anymore. He was Adam's brother, and I think Adam wants to talk about him, but he's afraid I'll freak out or something. Everyone treats me like I'm about to have a nervous breakdown or burst into tears. I know they think I should be over it by now."

"No one else gets to tell you how long to grieve."

Gage nods in agreement and then clears his throat again.

"He was really bright and warm, like you. He was made of color and light...until he wasn't."

The way he says it, I suddenly understand. His boyfriend didn't just die; he killed himself. It takes all my self-restraint not to come around the pool table and hug him until he's whole and happy.

"How long did it take you to stop picking up your phone to call or text him? I swear I still do it about once a week," I lament.

"That took a little over a year to break," Gage offers.

"Any day now, then," I laugh. "You know what the hardest part is?"

Gage's eyes meet mine, and my heart breaks for him all over again.

"That's easy, the hardest part is wanting to feel whole again but not wanting to move on. Because if you let go, who will be left holding on? And if no one is holding on, will the memory of that person just fade away?"

My throat tightens, and all I can do is nod in agreement. He nailed it.

"Can I ask you something?"

"Uh, sure," Gage agrees with a wariness in his tone that's endlessly endearing.

"Why the pink hair?"

Gage lets out a little huff of a laugh. "Believe it or not, there was once a time when I was fun, spontaneous, alive. Sometimes, I look in the mirror and see the flash of color and remember for a minute the person I used to be."

I have the overwhelming urge to hug him, but something tells me it wouldn't necessarily be welcome. He still wants to be that person, he just can't remember how. Gage needs someone to help him remember who the guy was before he was broken. I could be that person. If he lets me, I could help him put himself back together.

CHAPTER 7

Gage

My body is at Heathens Ink, but my mind is still at the bar two nights ago with Beck.

After the heavy conversation, I fell into an odd comfort, hanging out with Beck. We spent the rest of the night talking about easier topics like our friends, jobs, and favorite TV shows.

"Wow, that's different," Liam, Royal's younger brother, says, pulling me from my thoughts. I look over at him, standing in the entrance of Heathens with his camera around his neck.

"What's different?"

"Maybe it was a trick of the light, but I swear for a second you were *almost* smiling."

"No, I wasn't," I grunt, fixing my face into a scowl. If a man other than Johnny can make me smile, there's no telling what else he might be able to make me do.

"Hm, I don't know. The corner of your lip was ticked up and there was a little crinkle by the side of your eyes. Sounds like a near smile to me," Liam teases.

About a year ago, Liam turned up at Rainbow House, an LGBT+ youth center where all the guys and I volunteer. It turned out he'd managed to track down his long-lost half-brother, Royal, who never knew he had a sibling. Liam had been kicked out by their father when he found out Liam was transgender. So, Royal and his men welcomed Liam into their home and took over legal guardianship of him. Liam is the only one who spends as much time at Rainbow House as I do.

"Five bucks and you forget what you saw," I offer.

"Done," he agrees, holding his hand out eagerly.

I reach into my pocket and fish out the five-dollar bill I know is there and grudgingly shove it into Liam's outstretched hand.

"What brings you by?" I ask, already knowing the answer.

Liam's cheeks pink, and he looks down at his camera, fiddling with it and shifting on his feet.

"I wanted to show you some new pictures I took."

"Oh yeah? You must really like *me* to have come all the way down here," I tease.

"Liam, hey," Owen says with a bright smile, stepping in from his coffee run.

Liam's blush deepens, and I have to bite down on my lip to hide the amusement from my expression.

Liam has had a crush on Owen since he first laid eyes on him. Unfortunately for him, and much to Royal's dismay, Owen is a bit too old for him at this point at twenty-five to Liam's seventeen. But that doesn't stop Liam from swooning whenever Owen is around.

"What brings you by?" Owen asks the same question I did. This time Liam is even more flustered.

"I...um...have stuff...pictures. They're for Adam. I mean, they're for the advertising he wants to do to raise funds for Rainbow House."

"Nice." Owen smiles and reaches out to give Liam's shoulder a friendly squeeze. "I've gotta get set up for a client. I'll see you around, kid."

Liam flinches at being called a kid.

Is there anything worse than wanting someone who's outside of your reach?

Beck

"You were hardly even late today, I'm so proud of you," Clay teases, coming into Studio One to help me clean up after my mid-morning class.

"It was a fluke," I assure him with a laugh.

"I have no doubt," he says with a cheeky grin in my direction. "But I'm more interested in how your date went the other night."

"It wasn't a date," I correct. "It was just hanging out. Gage is a really nice guy."

"Does he...like you?" Clay asks cautiously.

I hate that this has become such a consistent topic of discussion. I wish the way I choose to dress didn't have to be this *thing* for people. But it is, which means, as my best friend, Clay is very protective about it.

A few years ago, when I was keeping myself buried under masculine clothes, I was dating this guy. Things were serious between us; I even thought he could be *the one.* We lived together, and all the signs pointed to a ring in the near future. Then one day, I grabbed his tablet to look up a recipe for a dinner I wanted to cook him, and I inadvertently stumbled on a string of emails that told me Dan was leaving me. He'd accepted a job in New York and was moving in less than a week. I felt like I'd been punched in the stomach. When I confronted him about it, asking whether he'd ever planned to tell me he was moving, he told me he'd originally planned to ask me to come with, but then he'd found my secret stash of high heels in the back of the closet. He said he couldn't see building a life with *someone like me.*

I was devastated and spent weeks crying to Clay and Bri, who both told me repeatedly that I could do better than a prick like Dan. After that they were both a lot more protective of me when it came to the men I dated, which weren't many. It didn't feel worth it to get my heart broken like that again, so I've kept my distance from anything deeper than the physical ever since.

A small part of me might have been hoping there could be something with Gage, but after the way he talked about Johnny, I knew I'd be competing with a perfect memory of the love of his life. No one can live up to that. I'll be happy with friends, and maybe a few benefits if he's down for that. But I won't give him my heart to break; it's already too fragile.

"He seems to like me. I mean, we're just friends, but he wasn't a dick about what I wore out to the bar."

Clay breathes a sigh of relief.

"I don't want to see you hurt again. You're awesome, and you deserve the best."

"Back at ya." I give my best friend a kiss on the cheek and then start getting ready for my early afternoon class to arrive shortly. "Don't forget Thirsty Thursday at O'Malley's tonight."

"Wouldn't miss it. I might even drag Max along. He needs to get out of the house more."

"Uh-huh," I mutter with a knowing smile.

Gage

The way the colors stand out against the olive skin tone of the woman I'm inking reminds me of the tattoo I did for Beck a few months ago.

As I lose myself in the process, my mind wanders to that day and how cute Beck was as he tried to hide his discomfort as I tattooed him. I've been itching to text him to hang out again since the other night. The feeling of *wanting* to spend time with a man, even in a platonic way, is unnerving. Cravings and desire faded so long ago, I was sure I wasn't capable of them anymore. Maybe that's why I want to be around Beck. Living again, no matter how slightly, feels *good*. It feels like waking up from a long sleep, refreshed and ready to face whatever the day has to offer. That doesn't make it any less unsettling. Being awake and alive, feeling anything, makes me vulnerable to feeling too much again.

After I finish the tattoo and take care of payment, I realize it's almost closing time. On Thursdays, the whole Heathens Ink crew goes to O'Malley's after work to unwind, so it doesn't surprise me when everyone starts to congregate around the front desk.

"Hey, did you ever call that guy?" Royal asks as Adam locks up and we all head down the block to the bar.

"He stopped by the shop a few days ago," Nox pipes in.

When I cast a glare at him, he shrinks against Adam's side with an apologetic smile.

"He did?" Adam asks with a surprised smile.

For a second I consider lying, but decide it's better to get the inquisition over with sooner than later.

"Yes, he did. He wanted to hang out, so we went out after work a few nights ago and grabbed a beer."

"That sounds like a date," Royal points out with a smirk. "Gage and Beck sitting in a tree..."

I growl and speed up my pace to get ahead of them. I need a fucking drink, *now*.

When we reach the bar, Thane and Zade are

already waiting for their men and saving us all a table. I make a beeline for the bar and greet Beau with a head nod.

"Beer?" Beau checks.

"No, I have a feeling I'm going to need something stronger tonight," I say as I glance back at my friends who are all talking excitedly and glancing in my direction. "It's going to be a long fucking night."

"Oh my god, Gage."

That voice sends a jolt of excitement through me before I can register and reel in the emotion.

I take a deep breath and glance over my shoulder to find Beck and another man standing behind me. The same hot, sick feeling I had when the bartender the other night was flirting with Beck hits me in the stomach again as I look over the man with him.

"This is my best friend, Clay," Beck introduces. I reluctantly offer my hand to the gorgeous man. Don't get me wrong: he has nothing on Beck, but he's certainly better looking than I am.

Clay takes my hand, eyeing me with speculation. Out of the corner of my eye, I'm able to see Beck, dressed in a flowy purple shirt and a pair of jeans that look as though they were painted on. For some reason, the flash of color from his toes makes me squeeze Clay's hand tighter in some sort of alpha male display. I'm not an alpha male, and even if I was, my forebrain can't work out a reason why I'd be acting this way right now. But my animal brain compels me to add a little sneer to my smile before releasing Clay's hand.

To my irritation, Clay looks like he's trying not to laugh, and Beck looks like he's desperately trying to be nonchalant.

"Did you come here to see me?" I ask suspiciously.

Beck bristles, his open smile instantly morphing into what I can only describe as a diva bitch glare.

"Excuse you. I'm not a stalker, fuck you very much. I came here with my best friend and his roommate to get a drink after work."

"Oh, right." I shrink back just a little, feeling stupid and a little disappointed. Some part of me *wanted* Beck to be here to see me.

"But it does look like your friends grabbed prime real estate; we wouldn't hate it if you let us join you." Beck's tone is softer this time.

I reach for the life preserver he's throwing me. I can invite him to hang out with me without admitting I crave his company.

"Yeah, come join us. I'm sure the guys are dying to see you and rib you about our date the other night." A teasing smile flits across Beck's face, and I realize my slip up. "What they think was a date," I correct.

Beck's smile widens, and he lifts his hands to his chest in a dramatic gesture. "Aw you really do like me. Don't you, boo?" he teases in a lilting voice. "Does this mean we're going steady?"

"Oh my god, how old are you?" I bite the inside of my cheek against the smile that's threatening.

Beck's response is to hold his middle finger up for me. The craziest urge roars through me for an instant. The desire to suck his finger into my mouth and run my tongue all over it.

I shake off the thought and nod toward the table for Beck and his friends to follow.

"Let us grab drinks, and we'll meet you over there."

Beck

"Damn, dude wants you," Clay says as soon as Gage is gone.

I turn toward the bartender to hide my smile from Clay.

"I don't know if he's even in a place *to* want, if that makes sense."

"I know you didn't miss how jealous he was. He nearly crushed my hand trying to stake his claim on you."

A little flutter of excitement flits through my chest before I can shove it away.

"Don't be stupid. Oh look, there's Max." I wave at Clay's roommate as he walks in.

I can see why Clay is crushing on him; he's like Jason Momoa in the flesh, all long, dark hair and intensely masculine features. He smiles when his gaze lands on Clay, and I can almost feel a spark between them. Yeah, I'm not sold on Max being straight.

"Do you want us to get lost so you can hang out with your man?" Clay asks.

"That would be weird. Plus, I wanted to hang out with you; getting to see Gage too is just a bonus."

We grab our drinks and make our way over to the table with all of Gage's friends.

"...So now out of nowhere the mother he's never even known is blowing up his phone, trying to tell him she's going to petition the courts to get custody back. He's freaking out, and I think we'd better check with our lawyer again and find out if there's anything we need to do."

I come in at the tail end of Royal's comment. The lawyer part of my brain instantly kicks in.

"If she abandoned him, that's a pretty clear-cut instance of involuntary termination of parental rights. Which means it's unlikely the courts will consider her custody plea," I offer.

Gage looks at me with shock.

"Really?" Royal perks up and lets out a relieved sigh. "That's fantastic news."

"We should still talk to our lawyer to be safe," Nash suggests before leaning in and giving Royal a quick kiss. Royal's other boyfriend, Zade gives each of them a kiss as well, and Royal seems visibly more relaxed now.

I glance over and notice Gage is still staring at me in awe.

"What? I uh...might have gone to law school," I mumble, hoping we can drop this subject quickly.

I don't know why, but for some reason, I don't want Gage to think of me as Beck the Lawyer. I much prefer him to see me as Beck the Dancer. I just want him to see the real me, not the mask I'm forced to wear.

"You just sounded smart and in charge."

"Are you saying I don't normally sound smart?" I challenge, raising an eyebrow at him.

"I'd have to know you a lot better to answer that question."

I roll my eyes and slide onto the seat beside Gage.

"When are you going to give up that excuse and admit that you think I'm cute and charming?"

Gage levels me with a look, but I can almost swear the side of his mouth twitches as he fights a smile.

"So why do you know so much about family law?" Zade asks.

"Max over there," I gesture to Clay's roommate, "needed help in a custody case for his daughter last year. His baby mama was withholding visitation without grounds."

Then I turn to Gage, desperate to change the subject.

Gage

"So, what do you like to do for fun?" Beck

asks.

A hint of panic flutters in my chest when I realize how blank my mind is in the face of that question. I'm trying to remember the last thing I did for *fun*. I try to remember what fun even feels like.

"How sad is it that I can't think of one thing I do for fun? I do things for distraction and to fill the day, not for pleasure."

To my surprise, rather than pity, I see a spark of challenge in Beck's eyes.

"We need to remedy that. Is there something you used to do for fun or are we starting from scratch?"

I strain my memory trying to come up with anything.

"I think we're starting from scratch," I admit in defeat.

"Okay, I'm going to come up with some activities, and we're going to try them. We're bound to find you a fun, new hobby. And, if all else fails, there's always sex."

I feel my face heat and my heart start to thud erratically as I force my expression to remain impassive. Beck enjoys getting me flustered. If I react, it will only encourage him.

"In my experience, sex isn't always that fun, either."

"Oh, sugar, then you're doing it wrong. I'd be happy to correct your technique, but let's start with some other activities and work our way up to the *really* fun stuff. Come by my place Saturday night; I have the perfect thing to start with."

"What if I already have plans on Saturday?" I challenge.

Beck arches an eyebrow at me. "I'll see you Saturday at six."

"Sure, why the fuck not," I concede. "Why are you doing this anyway? Why do you want to spend time with me?"

"Because, no matter how much you insist you don't know me, I happen to consider you a friend. Live with it."

After spending the next few hours encouraging Royal's taunting and Adam's hopeful smiles, Beck and his friends finally declare it's time to go home.

"I'll see you Saturday, and you'd better not stand me up," Beck warns before giving me a brief kiss on the cheek. It's no more than a brush of his lips, but the touch still ignites my skin in a long-forgotten way.

"Wouldn't dream of it," I assure him with humor in my tone.

Once they're gone, all the attention turns to me.

"Gage and Beck sitting in a tree..." Royal starts to sing-song again.

"We're friends, knock it off."

"Beck seems great," Adam says, his tone more cautious than I would've expected. I thought he'd be over the moon about me showing interest in a guy after all these years. Not that I'm *interested* in Beck. He's hot and fun to be around; that doesn't mean I'm picking out wedding invitations or anything.

"Yeah," I agree.

"Okay, I'm just going to come right out and ask," Adam says before taking a deep breath and looking me square in the eyes. "Beck seems nice, and I'd hate for him to get hurt because you're using him as a substitute for Johnny. I'm sure the makeup and the major femme vibe reminds you of him, and I get why you'd gravitate toward another guy like that—"

"Whoa, hold on." I put my hands up to halt his words. "Did you ever consider that I happen to have a type?"

"Oh?"

I shrug, feeling the tips of my ears heating.

"I *like* pretty guys, and I'm really into a man who looks good with makeup on."

"Oh." Adam's shoulders relax. "Okay then, good."

Then Adam's eyes light up, and I realize I just admitted I'm attracted to Beck.

"Shut up, it doesn't mean anything. He's hot, so what?"

"And you like being around him," Adam points out.

"So, what?" I snap again.

Adam shrugs, schooling his expression.

"So, nothing. I love you man." He slings an

arm over my shoulder and gives me a side hug.

I grumble and shove him away which only makes him laugh.

CHAPTER 8

Gage

Six o'clock on Saturday and I'm standing at Beck's front door, only somewhat less hesitant than the last time we hung out. I find myself wondering how he's going to be dressed tonight and if he's going to give up flirting if I continue to ignore it. I can't decide which answer I'm hoping for. It's kind of nice to have the attention of a cute guy. It's been a long time since anything has felt nice. Even if every bit of *nice* is tinged with the guilt of betraying Johnny.

I knock and the door flies open immediately.

"No false starts this time, I see we're making progress."

I grunt in response, refusing to let myself feel the odd little thrill in the pit of my stomach at the spark in Beck's eyes.

My eyes travel over him in what I hope is a discrete way, but the way Beck smirks tells me I've failed at being covert. He didn't give me a hint about what was on the agenda for tonight but Beck is dressed in a pair of skinny jeans and a band tee of some band I've never heard of. If it weren't for the makeup and the pink sandals proudly displaying his sparkly toes, I'd almost be disappointed.

"Are you ready to have the most fun ever?" Beck asks, impersonating a bad wedding DJ.

It takes more willpower than I thought I had to keep myself from laughing. But even without giving in, the buoyant feeling in my chest is a somewhat welcome change.

"Mmm," I finally offer a non-committal response.

"Just so you know, your dedication to resisting fun is only making this more enjoyable for me. By all means, continue to struggle."

"You're a fun rapist," I accuse.

"Yep, I'll shove a balloon animal right up your ass if I have to."

"Please tell me we're not going somewhere with balloon animals."

Beck laughs and leads me back outside.

"No balloon animals tonight. We're going to a concert over at the outdoor amphitheater."

"Oh, that's less dramatic than I expected from you," I admit.

"I told you, we're starting slow. I'm saving the live sex shows for week two or three."

"Good to know," I mumble.

"I love this place," Beck says, smiling and tilting his head back. "Have you been here before?"

I am sure my heart withered away years ago. But the way Beck's face glows from his smile, I could almost swear my heart is suddenly beating again. The lights from the stage dance across his skin, making his beauty almost ethereal. The gnawing need in the pit of my stomach is both unfamiliar and unwelcome. And yet, somehow, it's a relief to know I *am* still capable of feeling something after all this time.

"Dance with me." Beck holds his hand out to me. His eyes spark with amusement at what I'm sure is the obvious horror of my expression.

"I don't dance."

"Come on, you're supposed to be trying fun, new things. I'm not expecting Fred Astaire, just stand in my general vicinity and nod your head to the beat."

I sigh in resignation and take Beck's hand, refusing to notice how soft his skin is or how good it feels to touch someone, however casually.

Still clutching my hand, Beck starts to dance. He starts out tame, simply swaying to the music. But before long, he's spinning and shimmying like a ballerina on crack. Even being goofy and over the top, he's utterly graceful. And the joy in his expression is heartbreaking in its beauty.

When he spins out and then into my arms like a tango dancer, a laugh escapes from my chest, too full of warmth to contain it.

"You have a really nice laugh," Beck says, smiling up at me.

My heart thuds violently against my ribcage. Some long-forgotten place in my brain wakes up from its long slumber and starts to make irrational demands like *kiss him* and *make Beck mine.*

I pull my arms back, forcing a smile as blood rushes in my ears. Beck isn't mine. He can never be mine. I had someone who was mine, and I broke him beyond repair.

"I'm afraid I'm a bit rusty," I admit, chagrined.

"Never too late to pick it back up again," Beck reasons, stepping close again but not so close to warrant another retreat on my part.

His lips are rosy pink and so soft, slightly parted and unbelievably tempting. I can't remember if we were discussing laughing or kissing and I don't really care.

"For the first time in a long time, I'm starting to wonder if that's true." The hope my statement sparks in Beck's eyes forces me to backpedal as guilt washes over me. "It feels wrong to imagine happiness is possible, even in some vague, future way."

"I'm not going to give you any trite bullshit like saying *Johnny would've wanted you to be happy.* I didn't know Johnny, and even if I had, there's no way to know what he would've wanted because he's gone. But you're still here. You still have a life, a heart, and the right to be happy whether now or in a vague future." The way Beck holds my gaze is like a cobra ensnaring a mouse. "You don't need Johnny's permission to move on and be happy. You only need to give yourself permission."

I feel struck dumb by his words. No one has ever been so blunt about it before. Everyone has always tiptoed around the subject or tried to convince me Johnny would want the best for me.

"Thank you, I needed to hear that."

"No bullshit, that's what I'm here for," Beck assures me. "So, are you having fun?"

"Yeah," I admit somewhat reluctantly.

Beck studies me for a second before shaking his head.

"No, this isn't your thing. We can find something you'd have more fun doing. Leave it to me."

His voice dips a little at the end, giving me goosebumps. I force myself to put more space between us again. Something about the stars and the music and the way Beck's body beacons to me is all too much and not enough at the same time.

"Don't worry; I have the perfect idea for next weekend," Beck assures me.

"Sounds like a plan."

My apartment feels even emptier than usual when I get home from hanging out with Beck.

I glance around and note how cold it is compared to Beck's place. It's a great analogy for the two of us. I'm cold and empty, unwelcoming in every way, and Beck is warm and bright, drawing everyone to him without effort.

I strip out of my clothes and climb into the shower, needing the hot spray to relax the tension in my shoulders I've been carrying all night.

My brain can't make sense of the things I felt toward Beck tonight, but my dick has no problem making its own interpretation.

I soap my hands and move one to my already tight and aching balls and the other to my heavy cock.

I don't get laid often, which means jerking off is a matter of regular maintenance, so routine it's ceased to be very exciting or satisfying. But tonight, there's a fluttering heat in the pit of my stomach that isn't usually there.

Squeezing the base of my cock, I let out a low moan and then slowly stroke, adding a twist when I reach the tip. My knees quake at the overwhelming need boiling my blood.

My eyes drift closed, and the image of Beck kneeling before me fills my mind. His full red lips wrapped around my thick shaft, looking up at me through his long lashes. I have no doubt he buys the high-end makeup that doesn't run. But in my fantasy, there are lines of mascara streaking down his cheeks and my cock is stained red from his lipstick.

"Oh, Jesus," I gasp, placing a hand against the wall to steady myself as I pump harder, wishing for the heat of Beck's mouth instead of my own hand.

I imagine my fingers tangled in Beck's hair, forcing him to take my cock deeper in his throat and feeling his moans as I fuck his mouth.

A deep groan tears from my throat as waves of pleasure wash over me. My cum paints the shower wall as I gasp and grunt through the aftershocks.

Once my muscles stop trembling, I turn to face the shower head to rinse myself off, willing the debauched images to be washed away with my release.

CHAPTER 9

Beck

Sitting in a high-backed chair, with my back to my large Balsa wood desk, I ask myself for the millionth time why a successful career as a lawyer does nothing to make me happy. People dream of this life: thirty-one years old and soon to be a partner in a prestigious law firm, making heaps of money.

But all I can think is that I'd rather be dancing. I'd rather wear my makeup and high heels than an Armani suit.

This was Bri's favorite thing to argue about. She did everything to try to convince me not to go to law school. She knew this wasn't a life I wanted.

"Mr. Hoffman?" My secretary's voice crackles through the intercom on my desk phone.

"Yes, Elizabeth," I reply.

"Your father is on his way in."

"Thank you."

I sigh and turn back to my desk so I can pretend I was doing some work rather than staring out the window and fantasizing about never stepping foot in this damn office again.

"Becket," my father says seconds later as he

steps into my office without knocking.

"Father, what can I do for you this morning?"

"One of our larger clients, The McCullum Group, is facing a lawsuit from an employee claiming discrimination. I want you to take this one. It'll look good when I speak with the partners next month to show them you can handle our major clients."

I suppress a sigh as I reach for the paperwork he just plopped on my desk. A major client means a lot of late nights and extra hours to make sure everything moves quickly and smoothly.

"Thank you, sir."

"Just think, a partner before you're thirty-two."

I force a smile and try to remember why I didn't listen to Bri in the first place. After several seconds of awkward silence, my father turns and leaves me to look over the details of the lawsuit being filed against our client.

Me: Want to do that movie night we didn't get around to before?

Gage: sure, I'll bring snacks

Me: cool. I like nuts if that helps ;)

Gage: I'm not even going to respond to that

I chuckle to myself as I shove my phone into my gym bag.

"Are you even listening to me?" Clay accuses, arching one of his well-groomed eyebrows.

"Yes?"

Clay huffs in annoyance. "I was trying to tell you about this guy I met online; he might be the real deal."

"I hope so, you deserve the best, love." I pat Clay's arm, meaning every word while simultaneously not holding my breath for this guy to be any different than others.

Clay and I hit the treadmills, my mind vacillating between thinking of Gage and about the bullshit case my father dropped on my desk this morning. He had to have known how I'd feel about this case.

"Why are you so scowly?" Clay asks.

"My dad did something really dickish today."

I don't have to be looking at Clay to know he's rolling his eyes.

"What's new?" he says with more than a hint of sarcasm.

"This was really bad. He brought me a case, making a big deal about how much it will mean, showing the partners I can handle it, blah, blah, blah. Turns out it's a case brought against one of our clients for discrimination. The employee says he was repeatedly harassed and ultimately fired because he's gay."

"That's illegal, isn't it?"

"Unfortunately, it's not. That's the bullshit of it, this is going to be an easy case to win. According to the state of Washington, and the federal government, employees are protected from discrimination based on race, creed, color, national origin, sex, marital status or disability. But, not protected from being discriminated against based on sexual preference."

"What the actual fuck? Are you serious, people can still be fired for being gay?"

"Unfortunately. He might have a case for sexual harassment, so that might save his ass on this lawsuit. But how the fuck am I supposed to put my energy into winning this case for our client when it goes against everything I stand for?"

"Yeah, that's why I could never be a lawyer," Clay agrees.

I let out a long breath and crank up the speed on the treadmill to drown out my thoughts for a few minutes.

Gage

"Look at us hanging out and not even at a bar," Beck notes with a smirk.

"I think this is the start of a beautiful friendship," I deadpan.

"Aw, you really do like me," Beck teases.

I grunt a non-committal response.

"You're always grumpy. I bet it's because

you need to get laid," Beck taunts.

"You have no idea," I grumble.

Beck's eyes light up as he smiles and leans forward, hands on his chin like a teenage girl dying for gossip.

"How long?"

"Ugh," I groan. I eye him, trying to decide if he's going to drop this if I don't give an answer. All signs point to no. "Two years," I mumble as quickly as possible.

Beck's mouth falls open in horror.

"*Two* years?" He gasps. "Oh my god. This is a medical emergency. I'm going to have to perform mouth-to-cock resuscitation stat. Don't worry, I'm a trained professional."

"Don't rub it in," I grumble, and Beck opens his mouth to make what I assume would be a double entendre, but I rush on. "I know it's been way too long. I hate the whole hook-up thing, though. Those apps give me hives, and the club scene is like something out of my worst nightmare. My hand gets the job done fine, but sometimes you just crave the heat of another body against yours. Don't you?" Beck nods in agreement, studying me silently for a few seconds. "I hadn't been with anyone since Johnny, but two years ago I was so fucking lonely I thought maybe it would feel better to try."

"Did it?" Beck asks.

"No, it felt worse. Maybe it was because I didn't know them at all, maybe because they weren't Johnny. None of them were really my type. None of it was right, and I just felt so much worse after."

"We could, if you wanted to. It wouldn't be a big deal," he throws out casually.

"Could *what*?"

Beck cocks his head and purses his lips in disapproval of my ignorance.

"We could *fuck*," he clarifies.

My mouth opens and closes, no doubt making me look like a stupefied fish. *Is Beck joking?* I wait a few seconds, and when he doesn't yell *psych,* I start to consider the proposal.

There aren't a lot of reasons to turn him down. Beck is hot, and he seems fully capable of a no-strings arrangement. We're friends, but it's new enough that sex is unlikely to make it weird. Would it be so wrong to let off a little steam?

My mind fills with flash images of Beck and me naked, sweaty, and rutting against each other. I can almost feel his stiletto heels bruising the backs of my thighs as I fuck into his tight heat. My dick throbs in the confines of my jeans, urging me to agree to a night of wild passion, fuck whatever might come after.

But then the rational part of my brain pipes in and reminds me of the emptiness and guilt that had accompanied the few trysts I'd used to try to feel whole again.

"I don't think that's such a good idea," I finally say.

Beck gives me an easy smile and a friendly pat on the leg.

"Can't blame a guy for trying."

Then he settles back and starts watching the movie again. I don't know why a little bit of disappointment niggles at the back of my mind. It's not like I wanted him to try to convince me, right? I didn't want him to climb onto my lap, grind his hardening shaft against mine, and beg me to fuck him. That would've been awkward; I'm glad he brushed it off.

I glance at him and shift on the couch cushion. His face is relaxed as he chuckles and shoves a handful of popcorn in his mouth. Something deep in my chest aches in an unfamiliar way.

Beck casts his gaze my way again, his eyes warm and his expression full of light.

"This was one of Bri's favorite movies. When she first died, I tried to avoid anything that reminded me of her. Then, I realized *everything* reminds me of Bri, and I was fighting a losing battle. I'm glad now that I did because it's nice to be reminded of her in small ways."

I nod in understanding and then reach for his hand. It's just to comfort him and let him know I'm here. It doesn't mean anything more, even if it does feel nice to feel our fingers intertwined and see the appreciation in his eyes.

We could fuck.

The phrase replays itself in my mind on an endless loop as I lay in my dark, silent bedroom.

I can't decide if I'm the stupidest man alive for turning him down or if it really was for the best.

I toss and turn, unable to find the right position to shut my mind off and fall asleep.

We could fuck.

Jesus, his luscious lips forming those words was nothing short of torture.

I'm starting to think I was an idiot to turn him down. What could it have hurt? Am I really going to be celibate for the rest of my life? Am I not going to ever let myself have a single ounce of happiness for the next fifty or so years? If that's the case, I might as well be in the ground beside Johnny.

Maybe I could try to let go and see what might happen with Beck. Maybe I might even enjoy it.

That's my fear though, isn't it? I'm not afraid I'll hate fucking him. I'm afraid I'll like it too much.

Beck

"*We could fuck,*" I mock myself to Clay, who

snorts a laugh. "Dude, what the fuck is wrong with me?"

"You're hard up for a guy who isn't totally available?" Clay guesses unhelpfully.

"Pot meet kettle," I mock.

"Hey, Max is hot; that doesn't mean I'm hard up for him," Clay defends himself.

"Then why do all your dates go south so quickly?"

Clay flinches and then sighs.

"I don't want to talk about it. It's...not exactly a topic I want to discuss with someone I consider to be my brother."

"Sweetie, do you not remember that we've sucked each other off? We're not brothers, we're friends. If it's a freaky sex thing, you can totally tell me."

"That was a million years ago, Beck. I'd rather not talk about it. Can we please drop it?" Clay urges.

"Okay, sorry."

"This Gage thing? I think you shouldn't stress too much. You never know, he might come around. And if he doesn't, I think you're doing a nice thing by helping him through his pain."

Clay's words resound in me. He's right; I'm here to help Gage, not get into his pants. That is just a bonus.

Gage thinks he's broken beyond repair, but I've seen the hope shining behind his sad expression, and I know he desperately wants to be put back together.

"You're right; I shouldn't have put the moves on him anyway."

"It's been awhile since you've dated anyone seriously," Clay points out, and I tense.

"I think you know why that is."

"But does that make you happy? Maybe *you* should find someone you can get serious about? I remember before everything went to shit with that asshole ex, you seemed happy being half of a couple. I always thought you were a relationship kind of guy."

I huff in annoyance. Clay doesn't want to pick at his own painful scabs, but apparently, mine are fair game.

"Yes, I like being in a relationship, and maybe one day I'll meet someone who likes me for who I am. But until that happens, I'm fine being on my own."

CHAPTER 10

Gage

"Oh, man, you're not going to believe this," Adam says as we sit side by side, killing time at Heathens.

"It'd better not be about your sex life again," I warn.

"No, Cas stopped by yesterday to tell Nox that Harrison is dead."

"What?" A wave of relief goes through me knowing that the psycho who tried to kill Nox, and also murdered several other people in Chicago over the past few years, is now gone for good. "What happened?"

"Some prison yard brawl. I guess it was a wrong place at the wrong time thing, but I'm not going to shed a tear for him."

"Amen to that," I agree. "I bet Nox is relieved."

"Yeah," Adam agrees. "Maybe knowing Harrison can never get to him again will help him work past the nightmares."

I nod in agreement and look over at my best friend. I know he was just as affected by Johnny's death as I was, in a different way, obviously. And with the peace that seems to have settled over him since he fell for Nox, it's like he's a different person.

If I had a million years, I couldn't thank Nox enough for giving Adam the kind of closure and happiness he's given him.

I wonder what that must feel like and if I could ever have peace, too? Do I deserve soothing and happiness? Beck seems to think so.

My heart does a small somersault at the thought of Beck.

Beck, the crazy, beautiful man who demanded to be my friend and wouldn't take no for an answer. So why did he take no for an answer about the sex issue?

Wow, way to insinuate he should've raped you, I scold myself.

He offered, and I turned him down, end of story. Except it's not. Except I can't stop wondering what it would've been like if I'd given in and if that was a one-time offer.

"I need you," Beck says in a breathless voice as soon as I answer the phone.

"Uh..." I glance around to make sure no one is around to overhear. "Is this phone sex?" I whisper the last two words.

"What?" Beck sounds surprised and intrigued. "Do you *want* it to be phone sex? Because I can totally...wait, there's no time for that right now; I actually need a favor."

"Okay," I agree before I can think about it. It's not until the words are out of my mouth that I realize I didn't ask what the favor is.

"Seriously? Oh my god, thank you so much. I owe you epically for this."

My dick perks up at his declaration, and I have to shift in my seat to readjust. *He didn't mean anything by it,* I remind myself.

"What do you need?"

"I'm going to text you an address; meet me there at seven. I have to go, but seriously, thank you so much."

I'm having serious misgivings about agreeing to a favor without asking for details when I find myself standing outside a dance studio.

I let him distract me with a breathy phone sex voice; that was my first mistake. Before I can turn my ass around and start thinking up an excuse to bail, Clay spots me through the large front windows and waves me in.

"Hey, Beck is going to be so glad you made it. I told him after one too many jokes about my many failed dates that he could find a new dance partner for his class tonight. It may be harsh, but it's a lesson he needs to learn," Clay explains.

"Dance partner?" I repeat in a weak voice.

"Oh shit, he didn't tell you why you were coming?" Clay chuckles.

"No, I can't say he did. Is there still time for me to change my mind?"

"Nope, but you can probably trade this favor for some monumental gratitude." Clay winks, and I feel the tips of my ears heat at the implication.

"Good to know," I mumble.

"Yay, you're here. Come on, my class is waiting," Beck calls from down the hall, his head peeking out from a double door.

With a longing glance back at the exit door, I reluctantly head down the hall to make an ass of myself as Beck's dance partner.

"Sorry for the delay, folks, but my dance partner just arrived so we're going to get underway," I hear Beck announce as I push through the doors into the studio.

I glance around, noting that the room looks pretty much how I would've pictured it, with light wood floors, walls lined with mirrors, and an old boom box in the corner.

"Here he is; everyone welcome my friend, Gage."

I feel the tips of my ears heating as a dozen sets of eyes land on me. The class seems to be made up of middle aged couples of different varieties and two younger couples.

With a mumbled hello, I hurry over to Beck, undecided if I want to strangle him or do him this favor and demand repayment later.

"Don't be shy, sweetie," Beck whispers to me when I reach him.

I stand awkwardly beside Beck as he explains the dance he's going to demonstrate to his class.

When he turns toward me with his arms open, I swallow thickly.

"I don't know how to dance," I whisper in a panic.

"Just follow my lead."

I let Beck lead me in a waltz, stumbling and stepping on his feet throughout the instruction and muttering apologies.

Beck doesn't seem bothered though; he patiently coaxes me to relax and let him lead all the while calling out instructions to his students.

"You're doing fine," Beck assures me with a warm smile, and I stumble again over my feet.

"Sorry."

"You were right: you're a terrible dancer," Beck says with a laugh. "Lucky for you, I'm an excellent dance teacher. The problem is you're too stuck in your toppy ways. You have to let me be in charge for a change."

"Mmm," I grunt in response, imagining letting Beck be in control in all the ways he's implying.

I would've pegged him as a greedy bottom

all the way, but a little thrill goes through me, knowing he might also top on occasion.

I stumble again, cursing my distracting and ultimately fruitless thoughts.

Damn Beck all to hell for putting these thoughts in my head. Ever since last week when he asked if I wanted to fuck, I haven't been able to think of anything else. I've jerked off more this week than in the last nine years combined.

Mercifully, the class doesn't last much longer, and I don't think I inflicted any permanent damage on Beck's feet by stepping all over them.

I resume standing awkwardly as everyone filters out, many of them telling me what I good sport I was and thanking me for helping Beck tonight.

When they're all gone, Clay ducks his head in to ask Beck to lock up, and just like that, we're alone in the studio.

"Sorry I'm such a shitty dancer," I apologize, running a hand through my hair and trying to look anywhere but at Beck in his tight leggings that leave nothing to the imagination.

"You're not so bad, you just need more practice." He walks over to the light switches on the opposite end of the room and dims the lights. "Dance with me?"

Beck

Gage stands stiff and unsure. His jaw is tense, and his posture is ramrod straight. But to my surprise, he gives a small nod.

I crouch by my iPod and select *Cry to Me* from my Eighties Movies playlist. Yes, I love *Dirty Dancing*, no shame.

As the familiar beat fills the room, I swagger over to Gage. His arms hang at his sides as he stands stock still, clearly waiting for my instructions. I step in close and place my hands against his chest, feeling his heart flutter against my right palm before I slowly slide them up and around his neck.

"Try to relax and follow my lead."

Gage takes a deep breath and nods, his tightly coiled muscles relaxing and melting against me, his arms going around my waist.

He lets out a long breath that I imagine he's been holding since I turned down the lights, and I start to move to the music.

It only takes a few moments before he follows my lead. Gage's eyes lock on mine as we dip and sway.

I know I'm pushing it when I press the side of my face against his neck for a moment and inhale his scent. Affection and desire flutter in the pit of my stomach as Gage's hands clutch tight to the back of my shirt.

When I pull back, I can't resist a total Baby move, hitching one leg up and dipping back, forcing Gage to support me in his arms, one hand firmly on my thigh with the other holding my back.

"Warn a guy before you execute advanced moves, will you?" Gage gripes, but I can hear the humor in his tone.

"You didn't drop me," I point out as a joyful laugh trickles past my lips.

Electricity zaps between us everywhere our skin connects, and I'm certain Gage can feel it too.

I let Gage pull me back upright and find myself flush against him. I tilt my head a fraction of an inch, and our noses brush, our chests heaving against each other.

A slight tremor runs through Gage's body, and his breath hitches. Kissing him isn't an option anymore; it's a biological imperative.

I'm not sure who initiates it, but in a fraction of a heartbeat, my world narrows in on the way our lips and tongues clash in desperate hunger. A growl tears from Gage's chest as he crushes himself impossibly closer until I'm sure more of my weight is in his arms than on my own two feet. I nip and suck his bottom lip, eliciting a strangled moan. Of their own volition my hips thrust forward, grinding my hard, leaking cock against Gage's hip and his name falls from my lips.

Gage freezes, and my heart stutters to a painful stop.

He pulls back, his eyes wide with confusion and fear, his lips swollen and wet from our ravenous kissing. "I have to go."

CHAPTER 11

Gage

I kick my sheet off my bed and toss it to my other side in irritation. My dick is hard enough to pound nails only twenty minutes after my third jerk-off session of the night. It seems to have decided the only sufficient relief is inside Beck.

That kiss. *Fuck!* That kiss blew my mind and clearly my ability to see reason. His lips were even softer than I'd been imagining and infinitely more addicting. Now I can't stop imagining them everywhere. I want our naked flesh sweat slicked and sliding against each other. I want Beck moaning into my mouth as his cum floods between us, my dick buried deep in his ass.

A groan spills from my lips as my balls draw tight again, begging for release.

On impulse, I roll out of bed, urged on by the desperate, animal part of my brain seems capable of only chanting *Beck* and *need* over and over.

I tug on the first pair of basketball shorts my hands touch and then the white t-shirt I'd left hanging over my desk chair. I don't even bother with shoes, my sole focus being a few miles away.

It takes a few minutes for Beck to buzz me up to his apartment, but when I get up the stairs, he's waiting in his open door.

"What are you doing here? Is everything okay?" he asks. His eyes land on my bare feet, and he frowns.

I try to think past my lust fog to find words, but by the time I've stepped into his apartment, I still don't have anything eloquent or sweet to say.

"What you offered the other night, is that still on the table?" Beck's eyes widen in surprise. "Unless you were kidding?"

"Not kidding, just didn't expect you to show up here after midnight all sex crazed. Especially not after the way you bolted earlier." His concerned expression melts into excitement and hunger. "Hell yeah, let's do this."

Without further warning, Beck shoves me onto the couch and straddles me, his lips on mine. The warm weight of him in my lap goes straight to my already eager dick.

A deep rumble escapes my chest and is swallowed up by Beck's mouth. I clutch at the back of his shirt, burning with the need to get closer to him.

"Bedroom," Beck instructs between kisses.

Not needing to be told twice, I wrap my

arms around his waist and stand without pause.

"Jesus, He-Man, does all that pent up sexual frustration give you superhuman strength?"

"If that's the case, I should be Superman by now."

"Oh my god, was that a joke from Mr. Grouchy? My sexual resuscitation is working already!"

"Which one is your bedroom?" I ask as we reach a hallway with three doors.

"Second on the left," he instructs. I shove the slightly ajar door open with my foot, stride across the room, and toss Beck onto his bed. I'm on him before the bedsprings stop bouncing. I attack his mouth, trying to touch every inch of him at once.

Beck seems to be on the same page, making quick work of my clothes and then his own before I can even register what's happening.

My eyes wander over Beck's exposed body. He's so fucking beautiful, all smooth lines and edges. Unsurprisingly, all his body hair is neatly groomed. His cock is long and thin like the rest of him and so pretty, curving upward toward his navel.

Am I really going to do this? A hook-up with a stranger I'll never see again is one thing. But, I like Beck as a person. That feels like a betrayal of Johnny on some level.

Beck looks concerned as I slow and pull back, waiting for some sign from the universe that this isn't a huge mistake.

Beck's finger trails over the tattoo over my left pec, a heart with *Jay* in the center. When his eyes return to mine, they're filled with a shared sorrow.

"You deserve to be happy, Gage. Please, let me make you happy for just a few minutes."

And then my lips are on his, drinking in his goodness, light, and filthy moans. I grab his hips and flip us over so Beck is straddling me.

He kisses down my chest, and moments later, his lips wrap around the head of my cock, and his tongue laps at the bead of pre-cum forming there. Any thoughts of slowing things down or, god forbid, stopping are blown out of the water.

I look down to see his pretty red lips stretched around my shaft.

Huh, that lip color really stays put.

Beck looks up at me and winks before taking me all the way down his throat. The smooth muscles constrict around my cock and nearly drive me insane.

"Fuck, you have to stop or I'm gonna come," I warn, tugging on his hair so he gets the seriousness of the warning.

Beck releases my dick, but a string of saliva connects from the head of my cock to his bottom lip. The sight draws a whimper from me.

"Can't have that, can we Superman?"

Beck rolls toward the side of the bed and reaches into the nightstand. I take the opportunity to admire his perfectly sculpted ass.

Then a bright red color a few feet from the bed catches my eye. *Beck's red high heels.* My prior fantasy roars back to life. Who knows if I'll have a second chance for it? I stand and quickly grab the shoes before returning to the bed.

Beck quirks an eyebrow at me and smirks.

"Put these on," I instruct, trading him the shoes for the condom and lube he's holding.

"Kinky."

I tear open the condom and roll it on, coating it with a generous amount of lube and then adding more to my fingers to prep him.

As soon as he has the shoes on I stand at the foot of the bed and drag him toward me.

Beck lifts his ass up to give me access. My fingers wander from his taint into his crease, only just grazing his tight pucker on the first pass.

"Tease," Beck gasps.

"This is the first time I've gotten laid in two years; I'm not going to rush it."

I circle my middle finger around his rim, feeling his hole soften under my ministrations.

"How is taking it slow even an option after that long?" Beck muses, wrapping his legs around my thighs and dragging me closer.

I sink my finger into his hot depths, and we both moan.

"Please, I need your cock," he begs, testing the bounds of my self-control.

I hasten to add a second finger. I'm nothing if

not a conscientious lover...fuck buddy...whatever.

Beck bucks and pants as I fuck him with two fingers, wrapping my free hand around his cock and stroking him slowly.

"Oh Jesus. Oh fuck. Please Gage, for the love of god."

Deciding he's likely ready, I slide my fingers free and line up my cock.

Beck's high heels dig into my thighs, just as I imagined, as he tightens his legs, trying to force me to get on with it.

I press forward, eyes rolling back as Beck's tight heat engulfs me.

My muscles quake with the effort it takes to restrain myself and allow time for Beck to adjust.

When he grabs my ass and pulls me forward, that's all the encouragement I need. I slam my hips forward, grabbing him by the waist for leverage. His head lolls back, and he fists the sheets as pre-cum drips and pools on his stomach.

I pry one of my hands off his waist and wrap it around his cock. Beck lets out a satisfied cry, his channel squeezing me impossibly tighter.

I jack him in time with my punishing thrusts, and he begs for more. When I tilt his hips higher for a different angle, he lets out a strangled moan, and his cock pulses in my hand. I do it again, aiming for the same spot, and he comes apart, babbling incoherently, ass clenching rhythmically around my cock, ropes of thick cum spattering his stomach and chest.

I thrust twice more before I lose it, emptying myself buried deep inside Beck, collapsing forward and burying my face in his neck while my body is wracked with pleasure.

"Talk about unleashing the beast. I had no idea you had it in you," Beck pants when I roll off him.

"Fuck, I needed that," I mumble as exhaustion descends on me.

"Glad to be of service," Beck chuckles and gives me a pat on the ass before we both scoot up the bed so we can lay down properly.

My limbs feel like lead. I'm more relaxed than I've been in ages.

Beck's breathing turns slow and rhythmic, and then he starts to let out a cute little snuffly snore.

That's when it occurs to me I'm in an awkward situation. Spending the night isn't exactly good hook-up etiquette. However, sneaking out after fucking around with a friend seems like a dick move. And, I have no doubt if Beck wakes up and feels slighted about me being gone, he won't hesitate to storm down to Heathens and tell the world about my fuck and run.

I jostle around a bit as I get up, hoping it will wake Beck and resolve my dilemma.

"You leaving?" Beck asks in a sleepy voice.

"Yeah. We'll talk later. Sleep well." I lean over and brush a quick kiss to Beck's lips before I throw on my clothes and hurry out of the room.

Beck

As soon as I hear the front door close behind Gage I force myself to sit up and take off my Jimmy Choos.

Who knew Mr. Grouchy was hiding such a kinky sex beast under that broody exterior?

My muscles protest as I ease out of bed. I neatly set my shoes in their proper place and then head for the bathroom. A hot shower is in order.

As I step under the warm spray of water, I close my eyes and bask in the post sex glow radiating through me.

I can't remember the last time I was fucked that thoroughly. There's no way I can let that be a one and done. I'm not above begging. Pride is for people who haven't been fucked within an inch of their life by a surly tattoo artist.

I just can't fall in love with him. That shouldn't be a problem. Even if Gage's whole wounded soul thing pushes all my emotional buttons, I can keep this in perspective.

I learned a long time ago not to get my heart invested in a man. Even worse would be falling for a man whose heart already belongs to someone else.

Gage

I reach my car before the burning behind my eyes turns into silent tears streaming down my cheeks. My throat feels too tight and my skin is all wrong.

I wish I could say it's because I feel bad about what just happened with Beck. But it's so much more than that. I feel like I've been asleep for too long, and now that I'm awake, it's too much. I'm overwhelmed as everything crashes down around me and threatens to smother me.

I'd forgotten what it was like to feel anything other than shattered or numb.

It takes me several minutes to calm my breathing and get my wild emotions back under control.

It's not like I haven't fucked anyone since Johnny, but this was different. This was in a bed. This was with someone whose name I knew. This time I *felt* something. And I think Beck did, too.

I want to regret feeling something for Beck. I want to be indifferent or disgusted by what we did. I *don't* want to desperately crave the feeling of his skin on mine for a second time. I don't want to wonder if and when we can do it again.

CHAPTER 12

Beck

I wake up feeling pleasantly sore and unable to wipe the smile from my face. I sing and dance through my morning routine. And I let myself wonder when I can try to lure Gage over here for an encore.

Memories of last night are almost enough to make getting up for work bearable. *Almost.*

After I shower and shave, I shimmy into a pair of red lace panties and then pull my suit pants on over them.

My lace panties are my own private rebellion against my oppressive day job. I may not be able to wear my makeup, but at least I still have a small piece of myself on under my clothes. And maybe one of these days, I'll get the balls to quit all together and spend my days running On Point with Clay and never look wistfully at my coal eyeliner before leaving the house.

I glance at the clock and realize I barely have enough time to grab coffee before I have to meet with my client to go over the bullshit case I really don't want to defend.

Gage

I catch myself whistling as I walk into Heathens the morning after my night with Beck.

I hate to admit Beck was dead on that I needed to get laid. But a small part of me wonders if it was more than just getting laid. Sex with Beck was leagues better than any of the random hookups I'd tried. Maybe it was the shoe kink or the fact that I haven't let myself go for someone who is quite so accurately my type since Johnny.

Whatever the reason for the explosive chemistry, I need to figure out if that was a one-time thing for Beck or if he wants to make the benefits a routine part of our new friendship.

"Look at you, you're practically glowing," Royal notes as I pass his work space to get to my own. "Still claiming you and Beck are just friends?"

"We are just friends," I argue, hoping the heat at the tips of my ears doesn't betray me. It's not a lie; Beck and I agreed we were friends having a good time, nothing more.

"Riiiiight."

"Ugh, I need coffee," I announce, turning right back around to head over to the cafe down the street.

As I wait in line for coffee, I take in the pleasant rear view of the man in line ahead of me. His small frame and round ass remind me of Beck. But, he's dressed in a dark suit and dress shoes. All things I can't picture Beck being caught dead in. He's so much...*more*. He's bright and exciting. He's bursting with life and sex appeal. I rub my chest against the funny fluttering my heart seems to be doing all the sudden.

But then he turns his head, and I can see his profile.

"Beck?"

He turns around, looking surprised and a tad uncomfortable. His face has a washed-out appearance and his eyes seem tired.

"Hey, sweetie. How's your morning going?" he asks with a forced smile.

"Fine. Are you okay? Are you sick?"

"Such a sweet talker," Beck teases.

Before I can press him to give me a straight answer, his phone starts to buzz. He pulls it out of his pocket and grimaces before sending the call to voicemail.

"I've gotta go."

"Without coffee?"

"Apparently, liquid happy isn't in the cards this morning," Beck laments. "I'll talk to you later, sweets." He brushes a kiss to my cheek, and I can't miss the way his lips are a little rough this morning instead of smooth and slightly sticky like they were last night.

He's not wearing makeup. The realization hits me like a punch to the gut. Suddenly, a hundred memories flit through my mind of how many times I noticed Johnny had stopped dressing like himself and stopped wearing makeup. It's a catalogue of all the missed opportunities I had to realize something was wrong and get him help. The memories are an archive of my failures.

My stomach roils, and suddenly, coffee doesn't sound very appealing.

Beck

I rush into the restaurant where I'm scheduled to meet with Mr. Thompson, the COO of the McCullum Group, a financial analyst's firm and our biggest client.

I let out a sigh of relief when the hostess lets me know I've arrived before my client. If I fuck this up, I'll never hear the end of it from my father.

I order a cup of coffee while I wait and when a beefy, middle aged man approaches my table, led by the hostess, I stand to greet him.

"Mr. Thompson, pleasure to meet you."

"You as well, son. I appreciate you meeting with me so early; I have to catch a flight back to Texas in the afternoon."

"It's not a problem," I assure him.

Once we're seated, and Mr. Thompson has ordered some coffee and breakfast, I decide the best course of action is to dive right in.

"According to state and federal law, your former employee, Mr. Raleigh, doesn't have a case. My only concern is he might claim sexual harassment. Are there any incidents you can think of that he might be able to point to as evidence that he was harassed?" I ask, proud of myself for keeping my tone even.

"Are you asking me if someone groped the queer?"

I flinch and my jaw clenches.

"Sexual harassment comes in many forms. For example, if anyone made remarks about Mr. Raleigh's sex life that could constitute sexual harassment."

"Aw hell, I'll tell you exactly what I told *Mr. Raleigh*. The boardroom is like a locker room. Men talk, and if some queer is going to be uncomfortable with that, then he has no place there."

Smug satisfaction wars with nausea as I realize I won't be winning this case for The McCullum Group.

CHAPTER 13

Gage

A million stars twinkle in the vast expanse before my eyes. The heavy weight on my arm and chest is familiar as a long-forgotten sense of peace settles over me. I take a deep breath and let all the pain float away.

"This is so beautiful," Johnny says with a contented sigh, settling closer against me.

"It really is," I agree, tilting my head and brushing my lips against the top of his head. "You haven't visited me in a long time, Jay. I miss you."

"That's why I stopped. I want you to be happy. I don't want you to let your heart wither away."

I can't argue with him. My heart has been withering away. But when Beck smiled at me, I felt something for the first time in such a long time. It felt nice, but it also felt like a betrayal.

"What can I say that will convince you that you don't have to hold on to a promise you made a lifetime ago? If I couldn't give you forever, why are you so stubbornly trying to give it to me?"

"What if I can't love anyone else? Or, what if I do and something happens to him?"

"You can love. Beck could be the one to give you all the happiness I never could. He could be your fu-

ture, your forever."

I clutch Johnny closer to my chest. Loving some-one else would mean forgetting.

"No, it wouldn't," Johnny argues as if he can hear my thoughts. "Love isn't finite, G. I know you'll always love me, but it's time to let me go."

Before I can argue, the warm weight in my arms vanishes, and the stars blink out.

I startle awake, body sticky with sweat. I blink at the clock, feeling a heaviness in my chest that hasn't been there after a dream in a long time. I can't remember what I dreamed, but it's left me coiled tight.

For some reason, I reach for my phone, the urge to talk to Beck overwhelming.

It's not until it's ringing that I realize it's two in the morning, and he's likely asleep.

"Hello?" Beck asks in a confused, sleep rough voice.

It's such a sexy sound, it makes me wish I was in bed with him with our limbs tangled and a blanket shared between us.

"Hi, I'm sorry; I didn't mean to call so late. I'll talk to you tomorrow. I'm sorry."

"Wait, hold on," Beck rushes out before I can hang up. "What's wrong?"

I let out a long breath, scrubbing my hand against the rough stubble on my cheek and trying to figure out how to answer his question. What's wrong? *Nothing. Everything.*

"Do you ever dream about your sister?" I ask. I don't know why; it's been years since I've dreamed of Johnny. "Like, not a normal weird dream. But the kind where you could swear you had a real conversation with her?"

"Once, right after she died. We were in the bedroom we shared growing up, but we were both adults. And she told me I couldn't mope around. She said she was fine, and that I shouldn't take life for granted. When I woke up, I felt a sense of calm I didn't expect. I think she really did visit me in my sleep."

"You really believe that?" I ask, the hope and horror warring in my heart at the idea of Johnny still here but undetectable to me.

"Yeah, I do. I think they can't move on until they know the people they loved and left behind are going to be okay."

I swallow around the lump in my throat, trying to think of how to respond. Maybe he's right. Maybe Johnny can't move on just like I can't move on.

"You know, it won't be a betrayal if one day you *are* okay," Beck says softly.

"You sound like Adam."

"Adam must sound smart and handsome, then."

I laugh and some of the tension in my body starts to ease. How does Beck do that? How does he calm a part of my soul no one else has been able to reach?

K M Neuhold

"Do you need me, Gage? I can come over there if you don't want to be alone," Beck offers.

"I've been alone a long time."

"That doesn't mean you have to be forever."

I want to ask him to come over. I want to tell him that I haven't slept with a man in my arms for nine years, but with him I feel like I want to try. I want to tell him that just maybe I could find a way to put my heart back together if he can promise to be gentle with it. But I can't get any of those words out. Tonight, it's too raw and too jumbled.

"Not tonight, but thank you for the offer."

"Any time. Do you want to go back to sleep, or do you want me to stay on the phone?"

"Can you stay on the phone? Tell me what was going on with you this morning? I've been worrying about you all day."

"Aw, seriously?"

"Ugh, no, I'm half-asleep, nothing I say can be held against me."

Beck chuckles. "I didn't want to tell you this because I don't want you to see me this way…"

"You have some deep, dark secret? Intriguing. Do tell."

"Very deep and dark I'm afraid. I'm a lawyer," Beck admits.

"I kind of figured since you mentioned law school and knew about Washington state law on adoption. I wasn't sure if you were still practicing."

"Practicing and well on my way to becoming partner in my father's law firm." There's no enthusiasm in his tone, and when I picture him again the way he looked this morning in the coffee shop, I know that isn't the real Beck.

"Tell me about the peacock tattoo," I request, getting the sense there are pieces here to be put together.

"Bri used to always tell me I was a peacock and had no business trying to pass myself off as an ordinary cock."

A laugh bursts from me, and I can hear Beck laughing just as hard on the other end of the phone.

"Sounds like she had a way with words."

"That she did," Beck agrees with a wistful sigh. "She tried to talk me out of law school, and even after I went and took the Bar and started working for my father, she still told me almost daily that I could quit and pursue dancing. She wanted me to be happy. She always said life was too short; it turned out she was right."

Now I regret not having Beck here in my arms to comfort him, to find some way to soothe his loss.

"For what it's worth, I think she was right, but I also see the practical side of keeping a stable job."

"I'm miserable there," Beck confides. "But I don't want to disappoint my father and how do I walk away from a financially secure future like he's laying out on a silver platter for me?"

"I don't know."

"I think you would've liked Bri. She was so funny and sweet."

"Tell me more about her."

"What do you want to know?" Beck asks and then yawns.

"Everything."

CHAPTER 14

Gage

I wake up Saturday morning with nervous energy crackling along my skin.

I stubbornly keep my eyes closed, not wanting to open them and deal with the day. Although Beck and I have talked daily since last weekend—otherwise known as the night I lost my goddamn mind and gave into the most addicting pleasure I've ever experienced while simultaneously betraying Johnny—neither of us has mentioned what happened.

I don't know what Beck is expecting when I see him today. For that matter, I don't know what *I'm* expecting. It isn't surprising that my heart can want two different things so desperately; it's not difficult when it's in so many shards.

I want Beck to let me pretend nothing ever happened. I want him to continue turning himself into one of the best friends I've ever had and teaching me how to live again. I want to forget the mind melting pleasure our bodies shared.

I want Beck to throw himself at me the moment I step through his door. I want him to press his body against mine and tell me he can't forget, and we shouldn't resist the chemistry sizzling between us.

I pull the covers over my head and let out a frustrated scream into my pillow.

Reluctantly, I ease the blankets down and look at the framed photo of Johnny smiling at me from my bedside table. It was a picture we took during a trip to the beach our last summer together, a few short months before he left me broken. He looks so happy there, and I don't understand how he could've hidden his aching soul so well.

My mind wanders back over the past few weeks I've spent with Beck and the way he's drawn me out of myself and started to soothe some of my hurt. His energy is impossible to resist. I already feel things toward Beck. Not *love*, but something.

I close my eyes and remember the way my stomach swooped and fluttered when our lips met for the first time.

If I had never loved Johnny, I might be laying here right now giddy over the incredible man I could be starting a relationship with. I can see a world where I'd be lying in this exact position with a smile instead of clenching my jaw against impending tears. I can imagine the excitement and hope I'd be feeling as I'd wonder and daydream about what kind of future Beck and I could have.

But I don't know if my broken heart will be able to manage it now. And even if it could, can I risk the hurt all over again?

Johnny *did* exist, though. So how do I recon-
cile my love for him with the way I'm feeling for
Beck? Is this fair to either of them? Is it fair to me?

Beck

When Gage shows up at my apartment on
Saturday, it's all I can do not to launch myself at
him and beg him to fuck me again.

"Hey," he greets me with a casual head nod
that drives me crazy with how ambiguous it is.
Does he want a repeat or was that a one-time
thing? Does he regret it?

We've texted and spoke on the phone
throughout the week, but he's never brought up
the scorching night we had last weekend. And I
didn't have the balls to bring it up either. When
he called me in the middle of the night, I thought
it was for a booty call, but instead we just talked
until we both drifted off at some point still on the
phone.

"Give me a sec to change and we can go," I
say, gesturing to my yoga outfit I'm wearing.

"Do I get a hint about where we're going
today?" he asks as he follows me to my bedroom.

"Nope, no hint."

Gage settles onto my bed to wait while I
open my dresser to find something cute to wear.
Feeling the need for a confidence boost, I reach for
my favorite lacy jock. Once I've picked out all my
clothes, I shimmy out of my sweat pants, and I
hear Gage's breath hitch, and I smile to myself.

I didn't expect Gage to be so passionate between the sheets, and I've been craving him like crazy every waking moment.

I slip into my lacy jock and then turn around to face Gage, bracing for the possibility that lace might not do it for him. It doesn't matter; it makes *me* feel sexy. But it would be hot if he was into it, too.

Gage's pupils dilate and his lips part in a hungry expression as his eyes devour me. He swallows, and I watch as his Adam's apple bobs, waiting to hear what he thinks.

I can see the struggle going on behind his eyes, and I almost feel bad for tempting him. There's no question that he wants me. But Gage doesn't *want* to want me, and I shouldn't push him into something that doesn't make him happy. All I've been trying to do for weeks is make Gage happy. I can't ruin all the work I've put in by seducing him into misery.

I reach toward my pants, planning to quickly tug them on, planning to get dressed and then apologize to Gage for taking advantage of him. I'll promise him that I'll stop flirting and trying to get him into bed. We can be friends, *just* friends.

To my surprise, the war in his expression hardens into resolve, and he sits forward on the bed.

"Turn around," he instructs in a rough voice.

My heart leaps, and my breathing quickens. I do as he says, placing my hands on the dresser and bending forward for added effect. I have a great ass, and it looks even better in a jock. My cock is already straining, the smooth lace texture rubbing against my sensitive skin has my balls aching before Gage gets the chance to lay a hand on me.

The air shifts as Gage comes up behind me.

His first touch is nothing more than a gentle caress over my lower back. I shudder and press back toward him, seeking more contact.

"This is so...wow," Gage whispers.

His hands slide down to my ass and knead my cheeks. He lets out a quiet, shaky breath as cool air hits my now exposed hole. I can practically feel his gaze devouring me.

A gasp falls from my lips, and I wiggle my ass in his direction, desperately needing more.

Gage's lips brush against the back of my neck and I tremble at the sensation of a finger trailing down my crack and grazing over my hole.

"Please," I gasp.

"Please what?" Gage asks in a husky, teasing voice.

"Touch me."

I flex my hips, shivering with pleasure of scratchy lace against my erection.

Gage murmurs something I can't make out against my shoulder, snaking an arm around my waist and trailing his index finger slowly up the length of my erection, over the lace. I whimper at the teasing stroke.

"You like it?"

"Mmm," is his only response as he cups my balls and rolls them in his palm.

I thrust forward, continuing to revel in the sensation of the fabric against my skin.

"Can I..." Gage starts to ask but stops himself.

"Yes," I gasp, bending forward farther. I don't care how that question was going to end. Gage can do anything he wants to me.

Gage chuckles at my enthusiasm, but my pride is the last thing on my mind right now. The first thing is Gage eating my ass until I soak my lace panties with my cum.

He drops to his knees behind me, his hands grabbing the globes of my ass and massaging them, parting them, playing and torturing me until I'm panting and begging for his tongue.

His first kiss lands on the back of my left thigh just below where my leg meets my ass. His fingers trace the edges of the jock where it's held in place. His next kiss is higher, right around the middle of my left cheek. Then, the right cheek gets the same treatment. He continues placing chaste kisses around my cheeks and thighs until I'm sure I'm going to go insane with need.

When he finally parts my cheeks, I almost cry from relief.

"Mmm, such a sweet little hole you've got," he murmurs as he licks a stripe from my taint to my hole.

"Holy fuck, yes."

He gorges himself on my ass, licking and sucking and then fucking me with his tongue. He returns one hand to my balls, tugging and massaging them as they draw up tight to my body.

"More, please, oh god," I plead, thrashing under his mind-altering ministrations.

A finger from his free hand joins his tongue, slipping inside me and brushing against my prostate.

Heat flares in my lower abdomen, and it's nearly impossible to catch my breath.

"Right there," I encourage him. "Harder, please, fuck."

Gage obliges, adding a second finger, his tongue continuing to lick and suck my rim. I thrust back, impaling myself on his fingers hard and fast.

"Oh god, I'm coming," I cry as my cock pulses, hot, thick cum oozing out between the lace, my hole clenching around his fingers as I pant and gasp out my prolonged orgasm.

"Holy shit," Gage says when I collapse onto the floor next to him, my knees too shaky to continue to support my weight.

"I think that's my line, sugar."

His eyes catch on the cum soaked front of my jock, and his nostrils flare. He pushes my shoulder, and I lay down on the floor. Gage rears up on his knees, unbuttoning his pants in a hurry and whipping out his own desperate cock.

He groans as he wraps his fist around his erection and starts to jerk himself quickly. His chest rises and falls with rapid breaths, and his gaze never leaves the sticky mess I've made of my favorite panties. It only takes a few strokes before his mouth falls open on a guttural moan, and his orgasm shoots over my thighs and stomach, as well as adding to my own cooling release.

As his hand slows and his balls seem to be empty, he finally looks at my face again.

"Do you have more like this?"

"You really are a kinky bastard," I tease with a laugh. "It just so happens I have a fairly extensive lace collection. I have teddies and garters. I have thongs and jockstraps. I *even* have a corset. But you'll have to be a very good boy if you want to see me in them."

Gage whimpers, and my cock gives a valiant effort to revive quickly, to no avail.

"Let's stay in, and you can do a whole fashion show for me," he suggests.

"Mmm," I trail a finger along his stomach, watching as his muscles quiver under my touch. "Maybe next weekend. I already have something planned today, and you're going to have *fun*."

"This is fun," Gage argues.

"Told you," I crow before reaching down and giving his balls a gentle squeeze, more like a handshake than a sexual advance. "But there will be other days to explore all the joys sex has to offer."

As much as I want to give into Gage and stay here fucking all day, if I leave him wanting, maybe I'll buy an extra day of fooling around.

"Fine," Gage gives in, kissing my stomach one last time before getting to his feet and then holding a hand out to help me up.

"Give me a second to change...again." I peel off the sodden jock and toss it in my hamper and then grab a towel to clean myself off before putting on a fresh lacy jock. This time, I waste no time pulling on my jeans and a blue, frilly tank top.

When I turn back around, Gage is still looking at me with hunger. It's almost enough to convince me to stay home after all.

I shake it off and usher Gage toward the door before I can make a bad decision.

Once we're in the car, I tell Gage where we're going. "We're hitting the art museum today; have you been?"

"Uh, yeah, years ago."

"We're going to have so much fun," I insist, trying to get Gage excited about our outing.

He asked at the bar why I cared about finding him something he can do for fun, and the truth is I'm not sure. Maybe it's because he doesn't give out smiles very freely, but when he does, they light up his whole face. Maybe it's because I'm desperate for as much time with Gage as I can get before my dumb ass falls in love with someone who couldn't possibly love me back. Or maybe it's be-

K M Neuhold

cause if I can put his broken shards back together, then there might be hope for mine as well.

"I still think we would've had more fun staying home." Gage shoots me a playful scowl, and my heart leaps in my chest.

"I think I've created a monster. It seems my powers may be too strong for my own good."

"I haven't gotten laid in ages, excuse my enthusiasm."

"I'm a big fan of your enthusiasm. Museum first, then we'll grab dinner, and *then* we'll see just how enthusiastic you can be."

"You're on."

Gage

Knowing what Beck is wearing under his skinny jeans is enough to drive me half insane. As we walk through the art museum looking at masterpieces and odd modern art, I can't come close to understanding why I keep having the strange urge to reach for Beck's hand.

I shake off the impulse and listen to what Beck is saying about the piece we're standing in front of.

"Did you know when the Mona Lisa was stolen from the Louvre in 1911, the empty space it left on the wall attracted more visitors than the painting had."

"I didn't know that." I look at the picture again and think about his words. "It's sad that some things are more noticeable once they're

136

gone. You don't know what you have until it's gone."

Beck nods; the back of his hand brushes mine, and I almost reach out to knot our fingers together.

"Yeah," Beck says wistfully. "There are a million things I never realized I'd miss about Bri until she was gone. Like, she always used to call me during *The Bachelor* and give her running commentary. It annoyed the shit out of me at the time. I'd give anything now to hear her irritating opinion on a shitty television now."

The sadness in his voice snaps my resistance, and I reach for his hand, giving it a comforting squeeze to remind him he's not alone.

Beck gives me a surprised smile and squeezes back.

After spending the day with Beck, the confusion I was feeling when I woke up this morning has intensified tenfold. My mind is buzzing with every reason to let myself keep fooling around with Beck, as well as every contradiction.

"Do you want to come up?" Beck asks with a flirty smile.

My heart leaps with want, meanwhile my mind is racing.

"Do you mind if I take a raincheck?"

Beck's face falls, but he recovers quickly with a kiss to my cheek.

"No problem, sweetie. We're still on for next weekend, right?"

"Of course," I agree.

"Okay, I'll talk to you later then. Have a good night."

"Night."

After I leave Beck, I decide to head over to O'Malley's, desperately hoping that at least one of the guys is around and willing to help me sort out all this confusion. Hopefully not Royal because he'll have an absolute field day with this.

When I step into the bar, I don't see any of my friends, until I notice Cas sitting at the bar with a somewhat sad and wistful expression as he watches Beau flirt and laugh with another customer.

"Mind if I sit here?"

Cas looks over and gives me a friendly smile.

"Of course, have a seat." He assesses me with his penetrative gaze. "You look like you could use someone to talk to. I'm a good listener."

I take a deep breath as I try to decide where to start.

"Do you know about Johnny?" I ask and Cas shakes his head. "Johnny was Adam's little brother. I loved him so fucking much." My voice cracks.

I can't believe I'm saying these things to someone I hardly know, but before I can question it, the words tumble from me. I tell Cas all about Johnny and then about Beck. He listens thoughtfully, sipping his beer and nodding sympathetically.

When I finish, I accept a beer from Beau and take a long drink. Having spilled all the details, I feel less burdened, even if I still don't know what I want.

"You think letting yourself be with Beck is a betrayal of Johnny's memory?"

"Yes," I rasp, my hands trembling slightly as I absentmindedly use my finger to gather condensation from the bottle of beer in my hands. "I'm not saying I love Beck, but what if one day I did? Does that mean I didn't love Johnny? Or what if Beck falls in love with me, and I hurt him because I can't love him back."

"It's possible to love more than one person," Cas points out. "I know that from experience."

"Does it feel the same? Did you love both men the same?"

"Not exactly. It's the same thrilling, warm need to touch and kiss. It's the same desperate obsession with making him happy. But it doesn't feel exactly the same. How can it when the men are different, and I'm so different too?"

"What if I lead him on? What if I can't feel anything more than lust and friendship?"

Cas gives me a sad smile. "Don't you deserve a chance to find out? Maybe try living in the moment for a change and see what life has to give you."

I nod, feeling some of the anxious energy calm.

"Maybe I'll try that."

Beck

I'm tossing and turning in bed, wondering if I did something to upset Gage today. Or, maybe it's all too much for him. Am I pushing him too far, too fast?

My phone buzzes on my nightstand, and I leap to grab it.

Gage's name flashes across the screen, and my heart pounds. It's just as likely he's calling to tell me he doesn't want to hang out anymore as it is he's calling to say he changed his mind and wants to come back over.

I take a steadying breath and press the little green icon to accept the call.

"Hey, sweetie."

"Sorry, did I wake you?" Gage asks.

"Not at all." I lay back down with my phone to my ear and wiggle until I find the sweet spot. "What's up? Is everything okay?"

"Yeah, I just wanted to apologize for blowing you off after the museum. This is a little overwhelming for me. Numb was easy. Now, it's like I have too many emotions all the time. Does that make sense?"

"Yeah, it does. I'm proud of you for trying. I know it's easier to feel nothing than to face the pain."

"You've got that right." Gage lets out a long breath. "Can we talk for a little while?"

"Of course. What do you want to talk about?"

"I don't care; tell me a story," Gage requests with a chuckle.

"Okay, once upon a time there was a sad, pink haired prince…"

"Ha, I don't think that's a very interesting story."

"I don't know about that. Just wait until the part where the sad prince meets the knight in fabulous armor, and this story gets X-rated."

Gage laughs, and my heart flutters.

I'm in so much trouble with this man.

CHAPTER 15

Beck

"Why do you have a canvas bag with a sparkly dick on it?"

"I went through a bedazzling phase," I explain with a shrug.

"I'm sorry, but that's a major deal breaker for me. I don't think we can be friends anymore, let alone fool around."

"Shut your mouth, or I'm going to dig out my bedazzler and bedazzle everything you own."

Gage's warm laugh fills me up inside.

Over the past few weeks of messing around and doing fun things on the weekends, Gage seems to have relaxed and come out of his shell a bit. I have yet to find the thing he really enjoys doing, *besides me, wink, wink.* But the moments when I see a little bit of happiness shining past the pain makes everything worth it.

"Mercy." Gage holds his hands up in surrender. "Please don't bedazzle any of my stuff."

"I am a benevolent god, so I'll let you off the hook this time. You're lucky I'm feeling generous."

"I'll have to try to find some way to express my gratitude," Gage says in a low growl, giving me instant goosebumps. "What's the plan for today?"

I chuckle, not at the question, but at the tone in his voice that says he's wondering if he can distract me from whatever I have planned.

"We've been over this, activities first, sex after." Which sounds suspiciously like a date, but shut up, I'm not falling for him.

Gage is a sweet little bird with a broken wing, and I'm nursing him back to health. I know once he's healed and strong, I have to let him go. I *want* him to be able to fly; there's nothing sadder than a bird that can't fly.

I've always been a sucker for the wounded. I can still remember once, I couldn't have been more than five, when I saw a goose with a broken wing. I don't know if I realized at the time that his wing was broken. All I knew was that he was sad and alone at the pond with a wing that sat at a funny angle. I sobbed uncontrollably as Bri tried to comfort me, because I knew he was hurt and his flock had abandoned him.

Gage isn't the goose; he wasn't left behind by his flock. But his wing *is* broken, and he hasn't let anyone near to help it heal. Lucky for him I'm not good at taking *no* for an answer.

I slip on my shoes and turn to face Gage. Without warning, his arms go around my waist, and Gage pulls me close and nibbles at my bottom lip and then licks the abused flesh. A shiver runs up my spine, and I sink further into him as he plants several small kisses on my lips before leaning back.

"What was that for?" I ask when he releases me.

Gage shrugs. "Just really wanted to kiss you. Is that okay?"

"It's always okay."

Gage

"Let me just put on my makeup and then we can go."

A little shiver of desire gives me goose-bumps as I follow Beck to the small vanity against the far wall where he puts on makeup.

"You have a lot of different lip colors," I note in a casual tone. What I *really* want to ask is if any of it isn't so good at staying in place.

"Is that a problem?" Beck challenges, his expression hard like he's ready for a fight.

"Not at all. I love the way it draws attention to your full, soft lips."

"Are you saying you like my mouth?" Beck taunts playfully.

I grab a fistful of his hair and yank his head back to expose his throat. I can't resist nuzzling my nose against the crook of his neck and inhaling deeply before running my tongue along his pulse point. I lean close to his ear and whisper in a gravelly tone.

"Your mouth is an unholy temptation." Then I suck his bottom lip in and capture it between my teeth. Beck whimpers into my mouth and presses his erection against my hip.

The red lip stain is maddeningly still intact when I pull away.

"Let me show you just how good my mouth is," Beck suggests.

My stomach tightens and my nerve endings tingle at his offer. "Do you have any lipstick that doesn't stay put quite so well?"

Beck's eyebrows scrunch momentarily before understanding dawns in his eyes.

"I think I can find something that fits the bill. You'll have to let me go for a second though, sugar."

I didn't realize I was still tugging his hair. I release my grip and rub his scalp soothingly.

"I'm sorry, did I hurt you?"

"Don't be, I liked it." Beck's tongue darts out and swipes across my chin. "Don't move; I'll be right back."

I do as he says, waiting with a pounding pulse and an aching cock for him to return.

He's back less than a minute later with a tube of bright red lipstick in hand.

"Unzip your pants for me, baby. Nice and slow," Beck instructs.

I obey, my eyes never leaving his lips as he uncaps the lip color and begins to drag it over his bottom lip first, then the top. The motion is mesmerizing. Then, he brings his thumb to the corner of his bottom lip and smears the color just a little bit. A groan escapes my throat.

"Take your shirt off."

Again, I do as he says. My body hums with anticipation as I stand bare before him. Beck steps forward and presses a kiss to the middle of my chest. When he pulls back and I see a perfect mark left behind, my cock gives a mighty throb and my breath catches.

"Please."

Beck's eyes spark mischievously. He likes having me at his mercy.

He slowly lowers himself to his knees before me and looks up at me through his eyelashes. He takes my heavy erection in his hand and places a chaste kiss to the tip. My knees nearly buckle at the red mark he leaves behind as well as the drop of pre-cum that clings to his bottom lip when he pulls away.

I buck my hips, desperate for more, but Beck refuses to be rushed. He continues the torture of brief, seemingly innocent kisses all up and down my shaft, on each hip, on my thighs, and even my balls. Leaving red lip marks with each one.

I've never been this hard in my life, the crown of my dick turning a faint purple, and my balls so tight it's painful.

My lungs burn with the effort to get enough oxygen as he *finally* engulfs me in the wet heat of his mouth, sucking me down. Most of the lipstick has been rubbed off, but as his head bobs with each stroke, the marks he left previously smudge and smear.

"Fuck, that's so good," I gasp, unable to take my eyes off him.

The look of ecstasy on Beck's face as he slurps and sucks me is my ultimate undoing.

"I'm about to come," I warn, giving his hair another small tug in warning.

He takes me deeper, the tight ring of his throat constricting around the head of my cock and pushing me into oblivion. I buck my hips as I shoot down the back of his throat, my entire body pulsing with release.

He doesn't pull off until I'm drained and shaky, all my energy expelled through my cock.

"Now be a good boy and get cleaned up so we can go."

"I'm not sure if I've ever seen an indie film before," I muse as we search for seats in the busy theater.

"They're hit or miss, like anything else. But there's usually at least a few good ones at these festivals, and a few really weird ones that make it worth it."

Without thought, I reach for Beck's hand, telling myself it's because I don't want to lose him in the crowd.

His warm fingers are comforting, twined between mine.

Beck glances back at me, over his shoulder, and smiles. My heart flutters, and a smile tugs at the corner of my lips as well. I don't understand how he makes me feel this way.

"There's two seats together," Beck says, pointing at a spot a few rows ahead. "I'll grab those if you go grab us popcorn."

"Got it. Hope you like M&M's in your popcorn."

Beck stops and looks at me with surprise. "I love chocolate candy in my popcorn."

Such a small thing to get excited about, just another part of the spell Beck seems to be casting over me. His enthusiasm for everything is impossible to resist.

It hits me hard in the chest as I realize I am having *fun* just spending time with Beck. I want to be around him all the time.

How the fuck did that happen?

I spin quickly toward the concession stand and push through the throng of people, desperate for some fresh air.

I manage to get outside and take gulping breaths of the cool night air.

The memory of a night Johnny and I spent together before we started dating settles over me. We laughed and flirted while watching movies and sharing popcorn mixed with M&M's. That was the night I started having feelings for Johnny that were more than friendly. That was the first night I thought about kissing him.

Beck deserves so much better than to be relegated to fuck buddy for a broken man like me. Beck is light, happiness, and everything good in the world. Beck deserves to be loved and cherished every moment.

I want him to have all those things, but I don't want someone else to give it to him.

I know I can't be the man he deserves, but fuck if I don't want to.

"Am I allowed to want to love again?" I ask the quiet night, wishing like hell for a sign from Johnny to let me know what to do.

"Are you okay, sweetie?"

I look up and see Beck standing before me, looking concerned.

"Yeah, sorry, I got a little overwhelmed," I admit. "I had this memory of Johnny, and I just couldn't..."

Beck places a comforting hand on my shoulder.

"Do you want to tell me about it?"

I shake my head and straighten up.

"Nothing to tell. Sorry to leave you hanging waiting for popcorn."

I offer my hand to Beck, and for a second, he looks like he's going to argue or push me to open up more.

"Don't forget the candy," Beck settles for teasing, taking my proffered hand.

"I could never forget the candy."

CHAPTER 16

Beck

"How much do you love me?" Clay asks, giving me his most adorable smile.

"Bunches," I respond dutifully. "What do you need?"

"A little, tiny favor. It's microscopic, really."

"Tell me what it is already so I can start regretting agreeing to it," I prompt.

"I have this date tonight, but after the last asshole, I thought it'd be a lot safer to double date."

"Or not date guys you meet online," I suggest.

"I'll take it under advisement. But that still leaves me with tonight. Please, best friend in the whole world. Will you come on a double date?"

"Ugh, with the damn puppy dog eyes," I groan. It's not that I don't want to help Clay, but something about going on a date, even an obligatory, chaperone date, feels wrong.

"Oh shit, I forgot you have a boyfriend now. Damn, I'm not used to that."

"I don't have a boyfriend," I jump to correct him. If I let Clay start thinking of Gage as my boyfriend, I might get complacent and start thinking of him that way myself. In fact, there's a strong possibility I've already grown too attached. "Fine, I'll go on the date."

"Oh?" Clay blinks in surprise, and then his eyebrows scrunch together. "Are you sure?"

"Absolutely. You need me and I'm single, why wouldn't I help you?"

Clay looks like he's about to argue, but I fix him with a warning look, and he snaps his mouth shut.

"Awesome. I'll swing by your place at six forty-five and we'll go meet the guys."

"What's your deal?" my *date* asks, causing me to grit my teeth.

"What do you mean?" I feign innocence, earning a warning glance from Clay who seems to be faring slightly better with his date, so at least some good is coming from this.

"Like are you a drag queen or what?"

"No," I answer with a forced smile. "And before you ask, I'm not trans or confused either. I am a gay man who likes to wear makeup and high heels."

"Huh." My date makes a curious noise, and I'm about ready to start kicking Clay's shins under the table. How could he set me up with this guy?

"Are you ready to order?" Our waitress stops by and asks.

Clay opens his mouth to answer, but his date cuts him off, fixing him with a weird, stern look.

"He'll have the Tilapia."

I cut my gaze to Clay, feeling like I'm watch-ing a soap opera. Clay *hates* fish, and he hates con-trolling men even more.

"Excuse you, no I won't," Clay snaps at his date and then gives the waitress an apologetic smile and then orders a steak.

At least this disaster will come with some entertainment.

"I'll be honest, I don't get it. If I wanted to date someone in makeup and heels, I'd date a woman," my date muses.

I narrow my eyes at him and bite down hard on the inside of my cheek to keep from giving this asshole a piece of my mind. It's not worth the en-ergy.

I glance around the restaurant, desperate for anything to occupy my attention other than this train wreck of an obligation date.

My heart stops when I spot a familiar broody tattoo artist with pink hair. Even from across the room, I can see how deep his scowl is as his gaze darts between my date and me.

"Fuck me," I mutter. "Sorry Clay, I've gotta go."

The first step I take in Gage's direction sends

him out of the restaurant in a cloud of fury. Of course, I'd be wearing my skinny heeled pumps when I have to chase down my man. Wait...Gage isn't *my* man. I huff in irritation at my own wayward thoughts. Focus on fixing whatever is pissing off Gage now, then I can worry about the fact that I'm falling too hard and too fast for a man who's already been claimed by a ghost.

I manage to make it outside without twisting my ankle, and I find Gage raking his hands through his hair and grumbling to himself.

"Gage," I say his name as I approach him cautiously like he's a wild animal.

He stops pacing and looks over at me with sad eyes and a fake smile.

"Hey, I hope I didn't interrupt. I had no idea I'd run into you on a...date." Gage struggles with the last word like it's shards of glass in his mouth.

"You're jealous?" I ask with a mixture of surprise and a tiny bit of pleasure.

"I'm not jealous; you can date whoever you want. You're not a one-man kind of guy, I get that."

"What's that supposed to mean?" I bristle. "You think I'm some kind of cock slut?"

"No. I mean, you can be if you want, is what I'm saying. I don't own you. This is fun, nothing more."

The happiness I'd been feeling moments before has turned to shame and rage. How dare Gage accuse me of skanking around.

"I think this conversation is over for now

before *someone* says something they can't take back," I grit out through my teeth, clenching my fists so Gage can't see my trembling and realize just how his words are affecting me.

The god of best friends must be smiling down on me because Clay chooses that exact moment to storm out of the restaurant, nearly bowling me over.

"Oh, I thought you'd left."

"No, sorry to run off like that."

"It's fine; this date is a disaster. I'm cutting my losses. You need a ride?" Clay cuts his gaze to Gage, who's still scowling a few feet away.

"Yeah, I need a ride." And then I turn to Gage once more. "Call me when you pull your head out of your ass and you're ready to speak to me like an adult."

Gage

Sickening dread knots in my stomach as I watch Beck walk away from me.

In an instant, I'm a twenty-year-old kid again fighting with a boyfriend he didn't know he'd never hold again.

I lean over beside the building as dry heaves wrack my body, images of the last time I ever spoke to Johnny filling my mind. I thought there would be time to make things right. I thought it was a fight like any other fight that all couples have. *If I'd known…*

My phone rings in my pocket, startling me

out of my painful reminiscence. I rush to grab it, hoping it's Beck, calling to tell me he shouldn't have stormed off. But he had every right to storm off. I was acting like a complete dick. He's not the one calling.

I debate for a few seconds whether to send Liam to voicemail, but if there's a serious reason he's calling, I'd never forgive myself for ignoring it. Plus, maybe his teenage drama will help put things in perspective.

"Hello?" Even to my own ears my voice sounds strained.

"Hey, sorry I'm probably bothering you. Forget I called."

"Liam, wait!" I stand up from my hunched position, clutching my phone so hard I feel it nearly crunch in my hand. "What's wrong?"

"It's not a big deal. I just had a fight with Royal, and I thought..."

"Thought what?" I prompted.

"I needed someone to talk to. Zade and Nash just take Royal's side, no matter what, so I didn't know who..."

"I'm glad you called me. Where are you right now?"

"I'm near the house, I stormed out and just started walking," Liam admits.

"Okay, go to the park near the house, and I'll pick you up there. I'm going to call Royal and let him know you're okay so he doesn't worry, and then we'll go grab a bite to eat and talk. I've had a helluva night and could use a giant steak."

"Thanks, Gage."

"Don't mention it."

As soon as I hang up with Liam, I dial Royal.

"Yeah?" he answers, sounding distracted.

"Liam just called me."

"He did?" I can hear his sigh of relief through the phone.

"Is it Liam?" Nash asks in the background.

"It's Gage, but Liam called him," Royal says to Nash. "Is he okay? Where is he?"

"He's fine. I'm going to pick him up right now, and then I told him I'd take him to grab some food and we'd talk. It sounds like he just needs to vent to someone he doesn't share a roof with. If he needs to he can even crash at my place tonight, and I'll get him home to you in the morning."

"I don't think he took a jacket or anything with him. You can come and get his stuff if he's going to stay at your place overnight. He needs his toothbrush and pajamas," Royal fusses in a really sweet dad kind of way.

"Royal, don't worry about it. I promise I'll take care of everything."

"Thanks man, seriously."

"You don't have to thank me. We're family."

"Yeah, we are," Royal agrees with a hint of surprise.

I realize why he's shocked by my words. It's not because he hasn't loved me like a brother for years, but because I've always kept myself separate from the rest of them. I lived in isolation on pity island for too long. I don't know how Beck managed to lure me back to civilization, but it's way past time.

It takes me ten minutes to get to the park where I told Liam to wait. He's there, as promised, looking every bit of a seventeen-year-old kid, sitting on a swing, looking up at the stars.

It steals my breath to think that he's the same age Johnny was when he died. People take seventeen for granted, saying things like *you have your whole life ahead of you*. Maybe sometimes *your whole life* sounds a little too daunting to a kid who is struggling to find the emotional energy to make it until tomorrow.

Is Liam struggling the way Johnny did? Would we be able to tell if he was?

The statistic that hasn't stopped nagging me since I came to care about Liam like the little brother I never had, is that the suicide risk for a transgender teenager is more than double that of other teens. I promised myself that moment that I'd be there for Liam in any way he needed. I know he already has three men to care about and protect him, but it never hurts to have a spare.

"Hey, kid," I greet as I approach him.

"Hey old man," Liam mocks, rolling his eyes at me.

"Come on, I'm starving."

Liam climbs off the swing and follows me back to my car without a word.

"So, what are you and Royal fighting about?" I ask once we're in the car.

"He's being a controlling jerk," Liam gripes.

"Somehow, I feel like that's only half the story," I quip, ready to wait him out until he spills what's going down.

"It's stupid and embarrassing."

Rather than press him for details before he's ready to talk, we ride the rest of the way in silence to my favorite steak house.

My fingers itch to grab my phone and check for a call or text from Beck. But right now, I need to focus on helping Liam and living up to the promise I made myself to be there for him.

We both order a steak, and then the silence finally seems to get to Liam because he sighs and leans closer so he can talk quietly.

"We were arguing about surgery," Liam confides.

I frown. Royal and his men have been nothing but supportive of Liam.

"He doesn't want you to have the surgeries you want?"

"Not exactly..." Liam grabs a roll from the bread basket and starts tearing little pieces off without eating them. "It's complicated, but basically there are choices that have to be made with bottom surgery, and he thinks I'm making my choice for the wrong reason."

"Which would be?"

"God, this was embarrassing enough to talk

to Royal about."

"You don't have to tell me anything you're uncomfortable talking about. But it's difficult for me to give you advice if I don't know what the disagreement is about."

"Fine," Liam groans. "I want to get a full phalloplasty, but Royal thinks I haven't thought through the pros and cons of it. Apparently, he did his own research, and he thinks I might regret the fact that I would need an implant or a pump to get...*you know*."

"Uh, sorry, but I have no idea."

"An erection," Liam mumbles. "But, the other option would mean I could get a natural erection but it would be pretty small. What kind of guy would want to date me with a damn micro penis?"

"I understand."

"So, what do you think I should do?"

"I think you have to make that decision for yourself. And I'm sure whatever you choose, Royal, Nash, and Zade will be there to support you. But, I do agree with Royal that you should consider all the advantages and disadvantages of both. Unfortunately, neither option is perfect, so you need to take some time to think about which disadvantages you can live with and which you can't. I don't think this is a decision you should rush into."

"Easy for you to say. I'm not naive. I'm seventeen; I've seen plenty of porn, and I know how much people emphasize dick size."

"I can't believe I have to say this, but porn isn't real life. Real relationships are based on a lot more than a few inches between your legs."

Liam rolls his eyes again.

"Like what?" he challenges.

"Like shared interests and having fun together. Real relationships are about finding someone who is there to support you and lift you up, and put you back together when you're broken. It's your best friend who you can't stop kissing because you feel like you'll go insane if you can't be close."

"That sounds like love, not just a relationship."

Liam's words startle me because part of my brain sees the truth in his words while another part insists that I can't be describing love. I was talking about Beck, and I love Johnny.

"My point is, don't get caught up worrying about dick size."

Liam slumps back in his seat.

"I guess you're right. I just got so excited thinking about everything being *right* for the first time. I don't want to wait. I want to wake up tomorrow in the right body."

"I know, and we're all here to support you and help you get there."

"Thank you. I know I'm lucky having Royal, Nash, and Zade supporting me and making me feel safe. I know so many trans kids like me don't have any support at all. I shouldn't have been such a jerk to him when he was just worried about me."

"Something tells me he'll forgive you."

"Thanks, this helped."

"I'm always here for you, kid."

CHAPTER 17

Beck

"You think there's something wrong with us that we both go for all the wrong men?" I ask, passing the bottle of whiskey back to Clay.

He takes it from me and slouches back on my couch, considering my question as he drinks directly from the bottle.

"I'm not sure there is a *right* man out there for me," he laments.

"I wish you would tell me what's going on with you. Why the hell were you on a date with such an asshole in the first place? That guy can't possibly be your type."

"He's not; that's the whole problem."

"So, what, then?"

Clay takes a deep breath before taking another long swig and passing the bottle back to me.

"Have you heard about Shibari?"

I shake my head and regard my friend with interest. "That's not like an STD or something, is it?"

"Oh my god, you're so dumb," Clay laughs. "No, it's like bondage art."

"Bondage?" My interest peaks.

"Yeah." Clay swallows hard, his cheeks tinged pink as he picks at his fingernail and avoids my gaze. "There's an art to the way the knots are tied and the pressure points used to enhance pleasure. And I guess there's something to be said about the feeling of being held tight and surrendering to the pleasure." Clay shivers and then swallows again. "But, the thing is, it's starting to feel impossible to find a man who's into bondage without all the rest of the D/s stuff. I don't like pain or humiliation. And I sure as hell could never see having a D/s relationship outside the bedroom. So...there you have it; that's why I can't find a man."

"Wow." I blink a few times and try to get my head around it. I never would have guessed any of that. I have a million questions: like how did Clay figure out he was into being tied up, but I'm a bit too drunk to form them coherently.

"Are you totally weirded out now?" Clay asks.

"What? God no. I wear lace panties," I tell him with a shrug.

"I know," he laughs.

"There you go, everyone needs some kink in their life. The right guy is out there for you," I assure him.

Clay sighs but doesn't argue, he just lays his head on my shoulder, and we continue to pass the whiskey back and forth until the night grows fuzzy.

Gage

Helping Liam last night was enough to distract me. But in the cold light of morning, with no messages from Beck, I start to feel an edge of panic creeping in.

My mind travels back to the last night I ever saw Johnny alive. We fought and yelled, and when he climbed out of my car that night, I never dreamed it would be so final. If I'd known, I would've done a million things differently.

Knowing I was an asshole last night, I bite the bullet and dial his number.

My heart stills when it goes straight to voicemail.

My lungs constrict as I try to force myself not to imagine all the possible worst-case scenarios.

Beck

I wake up feeling grouchy and hungover.

I feel the bed shift behind me, and I glance over to see Clay passed out in bed beside me still fully clothed. I can't imagine that was a comfortable way to sleep, but I'm sure he was drunk enough last night that he didn't care.

I look around for my phone to see if I missed a call from Gage. It takes a few minutes of searching before I find my phone under my bed and completely dead.

"Fucking great," I mutter to myself.

With an irritated grumble, I plug my phone in and hurry to shower and get dressed. I'm already running late, and I know I'll never hear the end of it for being even five minutes late.

Once I'm showered, dressed, and shaved, I check my phone and don't see any missed calls or messages from Gage. It's still only at ten percent power because I have a shitty, cheap charger that takes forever when my phone is drained, so I leave it plugged in. Then, I leave a note for Clay telling him to help himself to whatever he finds in the kitchen and lock the door on his way out.

I bang my head against the headrest of my seat and wonder if it's too late to just back out of my parent's way too long driveway and skip our monthly brunch.

When Bri was alive this wasn't so bad. We'd ride together and talk about our week. Even though we called or saw each other daily as it was, there always seemed to be something to talk about on our drive over. She had a way of softening the blow of my father's disapproval, and would outright defend me if he got too harsh. Somehow, she never had the hang up about his approval that I seem to have been born with.

"God, I miss the hell you of you, Bri," I tell

the empty car. "Let's go hear about how I've disappointed him this month."

My mother greets me with a brief hug while my father offers me a simple nod of acknowledgment.

"I assume you're just wrapping up the account I gave you to handle?" my father asks before I'm even out of the foyer, and I feel myself tense.

"Just about," I lie.

"It's open and shut, if you ask me."

"Uh-huh." I don't trust myself to say more, or I'm liable to tell him what a prick he is for giving me this case to deal with.

Thankfully, conversation ceases as we sit down to a lovely spread, laid out by the housekeeper, no doubt.

The silence is deafening as we eat. I've long since given up trying to come up with something to talk about. I have nothing in common with my parents aside from working with my father. And the last thing I want to do is discuss work with him on a weekend...or ever, honestly.

"We need you to take anything you want of your sister's this week so we can donate the rest to charity," my mother says casually as she sips a mimosa.

My heart stills in my chest.

"What? Why? It's not like you can't afford to keep it in storage."

"It's not about affording it." My mother clucks her tongue in response. "It's time to move on. There's no use storing items for a person who very well can't come back to claim them."

Pain and anger swirl in my chest at her words and the cold way she delivers them.

"What is your problem?" I snap uncharacteristically as I shove back from the table. "It's like you don't even care Bri's gone."

"You're being dramatic," my father scolds.

"You want dramatic? Here you go." I give him the finger and storm out of the house.

When I get home, it's all I can do to grab Frodo's favorite blanket, the one that belonged to Bri, pull it over my head, and fall asleep in hopes the last twenty-four hours were all an annoying dream.

A frantic pounding on my door startles me awake. I look around my apartment in a groggy haze, trying to get my bearings. I have no idea what time it is or when I fell asleep on my couch, but the pounding at my door is getting louder.

I get up to look through the peephole and find Gage looking distraught. When I wrench the door open, he lets out a sound that I can only perceive as mix between a broken sob and a cry of relief. "You're okay?"

"Of course, I'm okay, why wouldn't I be?" I ask in confusion, stepping aside so he can come in.

He instantly pulls me into his arms, and it's then I realize he's trembling.

"It's okay. Shh baby, everything is all right," I whisper, rubbing soothing circles on his back.

Once he seems to calm down a little, I ease out of his arms and lead him to the couch.

"I'm sorry. Fuck, I'm a mess," Gage apologizes, taking a deep breath and giving me a sheepish look. "I'm so sorry I was an asshole last night. God, I'm glad you're okay."

"It's okay, did something happen?"

Gage rubs his hands over his face and then through his hair, leaving the hot pink strands standing up in every direction.

"I've never told anyone this, not even Adam."

"You don't have to tell me anything you're uncomfortable with," I assure him, putting a hand over his to let him know I'm here no matter what he decides to share.

"I was trying to call him that night. I called him over and over, but it kept going to voicemail. When you weren't answering, it triggered me or something. I'm sorry."

"You don't have to apologize. I'm sorry I didn't answer. I left my phone at home this morning, and then I fell asleep when I got home. Now, why don't you back up to the beginning of the Johnny story because I feel like I'm missing some of the details."

Gage takes a deep breath and then rests his

head on my shoulder before he continues.

"We'd been fighting a lot. I felt like something was off with Johnny, but I didn't know what at the time. All I knew was he wasn't the same person I'd fallen in love with. I figured it was because he was angry I wasn't ready to tell Adam about us. We argued over that a lot. He didn't want to hide, but I was afraid I'd lose my best friend for being with his little brother. We fought that night too. I told him he was being immature, and he didn't understand. I told him I wasn't sure I could be with him anymore unless things changed.

"I can still remember the way he went so still and the pain in his eyes when I suggested we break up. But he didn't argue, he didn't concede on his position. He just stormed out of my car, slamming the door behind him, and I drove home feeling pissed off and worried that I just threw away the best thing in my life."

A sob tears from Gage's throat, and he buries his face in my neck. I can feel the moisture of his tears as they hit my skin.

"It's okay; I've got you," I assure him, kissing the top of his head and holding him tight in my arms.

"An hour after I got home and calmed down, I started trying to call him. Every call went straight to voicemail and made me angrier. I told myself this was why a twenty-year-old shouldn't date a seventeen-year-old. I just kept thinking how immature and selfish he was and how maybe breaking up would be for the best," Gage continues, his whole body shivering once again. "Two hours later I got the call from Adam that Johnny was in the hospital. I never saw him alive again, and the last thing I ever said to him was that he was immature, and we shouldn't be together. If he thought I didn't love him, maybe that was the last straw. He was struggling with depression and drugs; maybe thinking I didn't want him anymore is what pushed him over the edge to take his life. What if it was all my fault?"

"Oh, baby," I coo in a soothing tone. "If that boy had eyes, there's no way he didn't know you loved him. Your love for him pours out of you every second. I know you don't want to hear it, but I'm not sure there's anything anyone could have done, short of a trained professional."

Gage nods against my shoulder and sniffles. "You're not the first person to tell me it wasn't my fault, but you're the first person I've believed."

"Why do you believe me?"

"Because you call me on bullshit. You always speak your mind. I know if it was my fault, you'd tell me without hesitation."

"Damn right," I agree, continuing to stroke his hair.

"Sorry, you probably think I'm a total head case."

"No, sweetie, I really don't. I'm sorry I worried you."

"I'm sorry I was a dick last night. I didn't like

seeing you with someone else, but that was my problem, not yours."

A flutter of hope expands in my chest. "It wasn't a real date. It was a chaperone date to help Clay out with a guy he'd met online."

"Oh." Gage nods and looks chagrined. "But, even if it was a real date, I didn't have a right to act that way."

"No, you didn't, and I appreciate you saying so. I haven't been seeing anyone else since we started fooling around."

Gage nods. "Me either. I guess that goes without saying due to my two year celibacy streak."

I chuckle and kiss the top of his head. "You know, being exclusive doesn't mean it's anything serious. We could agree that if we were going to see someone else we'd have to tell the other person first."

"Okay."

"Okay. Are you hungry or anything? I don't think I've eaten since this morning, so I could use some lunch or dinner...I have no idea what time it is."

"Come on, I'll buy you dinner to atone for crying all over you," Gage offers.

CHAPTER 18

Beck

It's nearly impossible to convince my heart not to get too attached when Gage seems just as content lying in bed, our limbs tangled, sharing lazy kisses as I am. His tongue drags against mine in a slow dance with no particular destination on the horizon.

Keeping things in perspective is a lot easier when we're tearing each other's clothes off like our lives depend on it.

But something seems to have shifted between us in the week since our fight and Gage's breakdown. And my treacherous heart is all too happy to kiss until our lips are swollen and sore.

Every so often our bodies align just right for a moment and one of us will let out a breathy moan.

"I didn't realize how much I missed kissing until you came along with your insanity inducing lips."

I chuckle as warmth settles in the pit of my stomach, not the tight heat that precedes the full body waves of pleasure Gage is so good at producing, but the pleasant warm tickle of giddy butterflies.

"You haven't kissed anyone since Johnny?" I ask mostly to remind myself why falling utterly in love with Gage is a terrible idea.

"Not like this. I'd kiss guys only as much as necessary to get off."

"How romantic." I try not to let myself get too carried away with a smug sense of self-satisfaction.

"It wasn't about romance," Gage points out.

"Neither is this." I don't know if this is another reminder for myself or a challenge. Part of me desperately wants him to correct me. He won't, I know that. But it doesn't stop my idiotic heart from hoping.

"Do you not *want* to kiss like this?" He moves to wriggle out of my grasp, but I tighten my hold.

"No, I do want this. It's nice." I pull back so I can see his face. "I'm just a little worried it's confusing things?"

"Confusing things how?" Gage frowns.

"Never mind. I'm being stupid; forget I said anything. Why don't we go out and do something fun today?" My enthusiasm sounds fake to my own ears, but Gage doesn't call me on it.

"Yeah, there's somewhere I thought I'd take you this weekend for a change."

"Oh yeah? Look at you, planning outings for us. You're like a real live person and everything."

"Yeah, I guess I am."

Gage

"Where are we?" Beck asks as we pull up in front of what would appear to the untrained eye to be a random warehouse.

"Rainbow House, it's the LGBT+ youth center and halfway house I volunteer at."

Beck's face lights up.

"This is awesome. How did I not know this existed?"

"It flies under the radar a bit, I think, to avoid any negative reactions from dickheads. They do such important work here, helping so many kids."

We head inside and are greeted by Mary, the matronly woman who basically takes care of everything at Rainbow House. She gives us both hugs and tells Beck she loves his shoes.

"I love this place!" Beck declares, and I smile.

Mary's eyes widen, and she puts a hand over her heart.

"Oh, my darling boy, I always knew you'd have a beautiful smile." My heart squeezes, and tears threaten from behind my eyes. Mary turns to Beck and puts a hand on his heart. "Keep him smiling, he deserves it."

"I'll do my best."

Mary nods, her expression serious, and then she gives me one more smile before she returns behind the desk and lets us enter to see the kids.

As usual, when I push through the double doors into the common room, teenagers are buzzing around doing various activities. I notice Liam over on one of the couches where some guys are playing video games. I notice he's holding hands with one of the other boys, and I quirk an eyebrow at him in question.

The last I'd heard, Royal was being a total grizzly about the idea of Liam dating anyone.

Liam blushes when he notices my questioning expression and gives me a look that begs me not to embarrass him.

I decide to be generous today and just tease the shit out of him later.

Without thought, I take Beck's hand and start leading him around to introduce him to all the familiar faces, meeting a few new kids myself.

t always breaks my heart how many kids and teens end up here. I'm glad Rainbow House exists, but I wish it didn't have to.

When we reach Kyle, I smile at how far he's come in the last year and a half. When Kyle first got here he'd been kicked out by his dad when he was caught wearing a skirt. He didn't want to talk to anyone the first week he was here, but then Madden showed up and bonded with him.

Kyle was confused and scared back then, not sure how he identified or who he was. But in his time at Rainbow House he's blossomed.

His eyes light up as he takes in Beck's high heels and makeup.

"Hi, I'm Beck."

"Kyle," he offers his hand, unable to tear his eyes away from Beck's style. "Are you...um...like trans or fluid?"

Beck gives him a patient smile. "No, I'm just a gay man who looks fucking good in heels and makeup."

Kyle's smile widens. "Really? Me too."

"Oh yeah?"

"Yeah. I haven't met anyone else like me here. I really like your makeup; could you show me how to do mine like that?"

"Absolutely."

I watch with pride as Beck lets himself be dragged off to give Kyle some makeup tips.

"This was such a great day. Thank you for taking me to Rainbow House. And you totally lied about not doing anything for fun. You love hanging out with those kids; it was written all over your face."

"Yeah, helping them does make me happy," I agree.

"I'd love to help them. I have to think there'd be some use for a lawyer around there," Beck muses.

"I'd think so. You should ask Mary when we go next time."

Beck nods in agreement and then takes my hand and leads me over to his couch.

"Can I get a few minutes of cuddles before you go home for the night?"

My heart squeezes in my chest. I let Beck position me like a giant teddy bear and then curl against me on the couch with a contented sigh.

"Mmmm, you're comfy and warm."

I chuckle and enjoy the fuzzy feeling thrumming through my veins.

This is so much more dangerous for my heart than fooling around. Sweet moments like this make me want to picture a future with Beck, where we come home to the same place at the end of the day and cuddle while we talk about how our days went. The little puffs of his breath against my neck get my dick hard, but also make me want to look at dogs to rescue with him and argue over where to go on vacation together. Beck's warm weight in my arms is planting crazy dreams in the barely mending pieces of my heart.

"Mmm," Beck murmurs again, this time pressing his erection against my hip.

I breathe a small sigh of relief. Sex I can handle, intimacy I can't.

"Sit up for me."

Beck groans at my request but complies. His eyes go wide when I roll off the couch and kneel in front of him.

"Stand up," I request and Beck complies.

I look up at Beck with a thrill of anticipation. My heart is pounding, my blood rushing in my ears. *My mouth is watering.* It's been so long since I've given head. I wasn't about to suck the dick of a random. But Beck—my beautiful, confusing lover—I'll happily suck him all day.

Beck's eyelids droop as I slowly unzip his jeans. I like looking up at him from my knees. He looks even better from down here.

Once his pants are open, I nuzzle the bulge in the front of his soft lace panties. I press my lips to the base of his cock through the lace, and Beck gasps, fingers threading through my hair and grabbing on.

I tug his panties down to his ankles to join his pants. His dripping erection is within licking distance, which is an opportunity I can't pass up.

I moan at the slightly salty taste of his skin and the heat bursting on my tongue. I trace every pulsing vein until Beck is bucking his hips and hissing curses at me.

"Please, fuck, please."

"Mmm," I murmur in reassurance.

I wrap my fist loosely around his shaft and slowly stroke him as I take his smooth balls into my mouth, and his grip in my hair tightens, stinging as he tugs.

Beck's pre-cum slicks my hand as I jerk him enough to make him crazy but not enough to get him off. I turn my head and kiss his upper thigh, sucking the skin between my teeth for just a few seconds.

He lets out a frustrated growl, and I chuckle against Beck's skin. Until his knee hits my shoulder, forcing my back to the ground.

My own erection flexes in my jeans as Beck hovers over me with his cock in his fist and an impatient scowl.

"Teasing time is over," he declares, positioning the head of his cock against my lips.

I open without hesitation, shaking with exhilaration for Beck to hold me down and fuck my mouth. I'm not sure where all these kinks were hiding before, or if Beck somehow created them in me. All I know is I want him in every filthy way I can imagine.

Beck's cock slides past my lips and lays heavy against my tongue as he rocks, building speed.

I lift my hands to his ass so I can feel the muscles tighten with each thrust down my throat. Everything about his toned legs and ass makes me desperate to feel him riding me. I can just imagine the way his hips will swivel in one of his graceful dances.

My fingers dig into his ass harder as Beck fucks my mouth with abandon. I want to taste his cum. I want to feel him shudder and pulse as he releases inside me.

I slip my thumb into the cleft of his ass and circle his tight hole.

"Oh god yeah, finger my ass so I can come," Beck pleads.

I massage with my thumb until he softens enough for me to push the tip inside. It's claimed by his tight heat.

Beck's movements become jerky, and his body starts to tremble. I hum around his cock and work my thumb in and out of his ass.

"*Gageyesyesfuckyes.*"

A splash of salty fluid hits my tongue, and I shove my head forward so he's engulfed deep in my throat. I feel every pulse on my tongue as he spends himself down my throat, his hips twitching and his breath ragged.

"Damn, you're good at that," Beck sighs as he flops down beside me on the floor.

"Glad to hear that even years out of practice I can still suck a mean dick."

"You definitely can. But if you feel you need to brush up, I'm willing to volunteer any time."

I chuckle, putting my arm around Beck's middle and tugging him closer to me. Beck nuzzles into the crook of my neck. I bury my nose in his hair and close my eyes, letting myself just appreciate the closeness between us. This is what I've been missing most since Johnny. The sex I was fine going without for the most part, but holding someone, being near someone, kissing someone, those are all things you can't fake or force.

"This is nice; I'm sleepy now," Beck murmurs against my skin.

"I should get going then and let you get some sleep."

Beck sits up and stretches his arms over his head. My arms feel empty as soon as he's gone.

"Just putting it out there, you're welcome to stay the night any time you'd like."

"Uh, thanks but I should go."

"Okay. Thanks for a great day." Beck leans down and presses a quick kiss to my lips before heaving himself to his feet.

"I think you could do a lot of good for the kids at Rainbow House."

"Thank you."

CHAPTER 19

Gage

The bell above the door sounds, drawing my attention. I look up to see a rugged man sauntering in. He looks like trouble with a square jaw dusted with stubble, a wolfish smile, and a few prison tats on his well-muscled arms.

"Can I help you?"

"I hope so. I was looking for Owen. Word on the street is that he works here?"

"Oh? Yeah, Owen works here." It's not like I know much of Owen's backstory, but I never pictured him spending time around a guy like this. "Let me check if he's free."

I make my way back to Owen's work space and knock on the door.

"Come in."

"Hey, man, there's some guy here looking for you."

"Some guy?" Owen cocks his head. "What does he look like?"

"Like he just got out of prison."

Owen's face pales a little, and his smile turns into more of a grimace.

"Okay, cool. Tell him I'll be right up."

I nod and head back up front to find the man loitering about, looking anxious.

"Owen said he'll be right up."

The man breathes a sigh of relief.

"Thanks."

I spend the next few minutes pretending to work on the computer while keeping an eye on the man out of the corner of my eye. He doesn't seem like someone Owen would know or spend time with. Then again, I don't know Owen very well. Maybe this is exactly the kind of person Owen usually hangs out with.

Based on the nervous fidgeting, I wonder if he's an ex-boyfriend of Owen's.

Owen finally appears from the back with a wary expression.

He draws up short when he sees the man before a wide smile spreads across his face.

"Rollins? Holy shit, dude." Owen strides forward and the other man—*Rollins*?—stands, giving Owen a surprised smile in return.

"I actually go by Finn when I'm outside the —"

"Got it," Owen cuts him off and casts a quick glance at me.

Finn's eyes cut to me as well with a look of understanding before he offers his fist for a bump to Owen.

"I hope it's okay I came looking for you. I was wondering if you'd want to grab a drink or anything and catch up?"

I know I shouldn't be eavesdropping, but the curiosity is killing me. There's subtext to the invitation I can't begin to unravel.

"I'd love to. Let me jot my number for you and you can text me to make plans."

Finn leaves a few minutes later, and Owen returns to his work space without any kind of explanation.

"Want to grab lunch?" Adam asks after his eleven a.m. appointment.

"Yeah," I agree, putting aside the sketch I'm working on and standing up to stretch.

Adam slings an arm over my shoulder, and we head out.

"Hey, you know what I've been thinking? We should plan a bachelor party for Madden and Thane now that they've set a date for the wedding," I suggest.

Adam draws up short, and I turn to see him looking surprised.

"What did you have in mind?" he asks after a few moments of confused silence.

"Um..." I rub the back of my neck, suddenly self-conscious. "I thought Vegas would be fun."

He blinks a few times, looking at me like he's trying to figure out who I am.

"That's an awesome idea. Let's get together

with Royal, Zade, Nash, and Dani to plan it."

"Cool," I say with relief.

"I'd love to get to know Beck better; do you think we could do a double date?"

I cock my head at his strange non-sequitur.

"We're not really *dating*," I hedge.

"The four of us could hang out, couldn't we? It doesn't have to be high pressure or anything, just a few drinks."

"Yeah, we can do that. I'll check with Beck, and maybe we can get together this weekend."

Adam claps me on the back, and we start walking again.

Beck

I'm sitting at my desk daydreaming about what type of fun activity I want to inflict on Gage this weekend when my father strides into my office without so much as a knock.

"Becket, would you care to explain to me why you told the McCullum Group they need to offer a settlement to the employee who was let go?"

"Because offering a settlement is often less costly and easier to shield from public scrutiny than going to trial."

"Cute," my father sneers. "That employee doesn't have a case. You and I both know the law is on our client's side."

"In regards to the fact that sexual orientation isn't covered in cases of discrimination, yes.

But there is still a clear case for sexual harassment. The employee was made to feel uncomfortable due to sexually explicit comments made in the workplace, which affected his ability to do his job."

My father's jaw clenches, and a little vein in his neck pulses.

"That's hard to prove and you know it. Find a more favorable outcome for this client so the partners will be happy and do it now. Are we clear?"

I bite my tongue against all the things I want to say to him. In the back of my mind, I can hear Bri telling me to call him a self-centered prick. Instead, I simply nod and watch as he storms out of my office as quickly as he arrived.

Anger and shame simmer in my gut for the rest of the day. And by the time I meet Clay at our weekly pole dancing class, I'm shaking and fuming, my thoughts going in too many directions at once.

"Whoa, babe. What's wrong?"

"My father," I bite out before changing into my pole dancing clothes and heading into the studio with Clay on my heels.

"Do you want to talk about it?" he offers as we start to stretch.

"Not right now." All I want is to work up a sweat and forget about all the bullshit.

By the end of class, my muscles are trembling with exertion, and my skin is slicked with sweat. All I can think about is calling Gage and begging him to come over and help me work out the remains of my frustration.

To my surprise, when Clay and I get back to the locker room to change, I find a missed call from Gage.

I call him back while I slip out of my sparkly spandex shorts and rummage in my bag for a towel to wipe off some of the sweat.

"Hey," Gage answers after two rings.

"Hey, baby, what's up?"

"Bored and restless tonight so I thought I'd see what you were up to."

A smile breaks out across my lips. I was the first person Gage thought of when he wanted to get out of the house.

"I'm finishing up at my pole dancing class; meet me at my place in twenty minutes?"

"Pole dancing?" Gage's voice takes on a deep husky tone, and I imagine his cock thickening and the tips of his ear pinking with arousal.

"Mmhmm, maybe I can give you a demonstration sometime."

Gage makes a strangled noise and I chuckle.

"See you in twenty, sweetheart."

I toss my phone back into my bag and finish toweling off.

"You're really into him."

I bristle at Clay's words. "No, I'm not. He's a friend, and we fool around, no big deal."

"Uh-huh. I seem to remember that when *we* were friends who fooled around, you were over it after a few handjobs."

"That's not fair; you weren't into it either."

"Yeah, but that's for different reasons, you know that."

"I know," I assure him. "You and I don't have chemistry like that. Gage and I are explosive, but that doesn't mean it's serious or that I can afford to get attached. His heart isn't available, and that's okay."

"Is it?" Clay eyes me with disbelief. "I don't want your heart broken."

"Eh," I shrug. "Sometimes heartbreak is worth it. I'm a big boy; I can handle it."

"Okay, I just love you and hate seeing you hurt."

"Love you, too." I give Clay a kiss on the cheek and then tug my shirt over my head and fling my bag over my shoulder. "I'll see you later."

Gage is waiting outside my building when I get home.

"Hope it's okay I called you to hang out?"

"Of course, you're always welcome. It's nice

not to be alone in my apartment at the end of the day."

"Yeah," Gage agrees. "I never thought it would be so damn *quiet* living alone. Sometimes I feel like I'm about to crawl out of my skin."

I nod in agreement and lead Gage up to my place.

"I never wanted to live alone. I'd spent so much time imagining moving in with Johnny eventually, when he died the dream of someone to call my own and share my life with died with him. But I think that hopeless romantic might still be in there somewhere because I really hate my empty apartment now."

Gage's confession makes me want to cry for him. He has so much love to give, if he could just let go enough to share his fragile heart.

"I know what you mean. I had a bad relationship a few years back, and since then, I've stuck to casual, but I do miss sharing my bed some nights."

Gage bites down on his bottom lip and then looks at me cautiously. "Maybe I could stay the night tonight?" His question is so quiet I almost ask him to repeat it so I can be sure I haven't misheard.

"I'd like that."

Gage's shoulders relax and he gives me a tentative smile.

I sit down on the couch and pat the cushion beside me. "Tell me about your day," I request.

An array of emotions plays over Gage's face for a few seconds, and I'm not sure if he's going to cry, run away, or kiss me. Finally, he sits beside me and pulls me against his chest so we can lay together on the couch.

"My day was weird. Some random dude showed up to talk to Owen, and it was awkward, so I'm thinking maybe it's his ex or something? Oh, and then Adam suggested you and I do something with him and Nox? He said he'd like to get to know you more."

"I'd like that." I do my best to keep my voice even so I don't give away how many things I'm feeling knowing Gage wants me to get to know his best friend better.

"Cool, I'll let him know you're up for it." Gage buries his nose in my hair for a second, his breath ruffling the top of my head and beckoning me closer. "How was your day?"

"Craptastic," I admit. As much as I didn't want to talk to Clay about the bullshit with my father, I can't imagine *not* sharing it with Gage. I let him in on the case I was given and how it's played out so far. "Before I left for the day, I got an email to meet with the partners tomorrow to let them know how the case is resolving."

"That's bullshit," Gage sympathizes.

"Yeah. I don't know what I'm supposed to do. The worst part is I can imagine what Bri would say if she was here. She'd be pushing me to tell him where to shove it. Maybe I should quit this stupid fucking job and spend my time doing something useful instead."

"I think you should do whatever will make you happy."

"Thanks," I sigh and snuggle closer to Gage. "Want to watch a movie or something and then go to bed?"

"That sounds nice," Gage agrees as his hand caresses my back.

Gage

"I have a spare toothbrush under the sink," Beck offers as I head into the bathroom to get ready for bed.

After washing my face and finding the fresh toothbrush under the sink, I start to search around for toothpaste. I open the medicine cabinet, and my breath catches. I stare at the orange prescription bottle unblinking for several long seconds.

I know I should respect his privacy, but I can't keep myself from reaching for the bottle with a trembling hand. I have to know if it's something stupid like antibiotics or if I need to be concerned. I'm already getting in too deep with Beck, and my heart can't take another blow.

"Gage, is everything okay?" Beck calls through the door.

I pull my hand back at lightning speed, excuses forming on my lips.

"Uh..."

"I'm coming in," Beck warns, and seconds later, the door opens.

"I wasn't snooping. I was looking for toothpaste," I blurt.

Beck's eyes flick between me and the open cabinet.

"They're anti-depressants," Beck explains without hesitation.

My blood turns to ice in my veins. "You're depressed?" I ask in a shaky whisper.

Beck steps close and wraps his arms around my middle.

"No, baby," Beck assures me. "I got those after Bri died, and I was having trouble coping. I was weaned off a few months ago. I'm okay, I promise you."

"I can't handle losing someone again," I murmur against Beck's neck, hugging him as close as I can manage.

"I know." Beck rubs a soothing circle between my shoulder blades. "Let's go to bed."

I kiss along his neck and then nibble his jaw when I reach it. "Yeah, let's go to bed," I agree.

CHAPTER 20

Gage

The warm presence of a body curled against my back sets my heart thundering before I even open my eyes.

The warmth of shared heat under the covers and the smooth legs brushing against mine makes my morning erection pulse and my body shiver.

I forgot how nice it is to share a bed with someone. Not just anyone, because I can't imagine how sick I would feel waking up beside a stranger. But Beck isn't a stranger. Beck is my best friend and my fucking savior. I can't begin to sort out all the fuzzy feelings I'm starting to associate with Beck, but all I want is to be near him all the time.

Last night, I'd been moping around my empty home, feeling sorry for myself, when it occurred to me to stop pussyfooting around and just call Beck.

I didn't plan to spend the night, but when he mentioned how lonely his bed gets at night, I couldn't find an ounce of resistance within me.

"Mmm, you smell nice in the morning," Beck murmurs against my shoulder and then places several kisses there.

I chuckle. "I smell different in the morning?"

"Mmmhmm, you smell all warm and like Gage, but also a little like me from sleeping in my bed." Beck lifts my arm and burrows under it; he buries his nose in my armpit and inhales and then licks my ribcage.

I flex my hips, my cock leaking onto his sheets, my balls tight and heavy. "How do you feel about morning sex?"

"Very pro, however, I have to get to work so that'll have to wait until a different day."

Beck gives me one more quick kiss on the side of the neck before slipping out of bed, unfortunately not thwarted by my arms tightening around him and attempting to keep him from leaving.

I roll onto my back and watch as Beck pulls clothes out of his dresser and then goes to his closet for a suit.

My mouth waters as I watch Beck give his cock a few lazy strokes before tucking it against his hip, held in place by his lacy pink panties.

"Fuck, that's hot."

"Mmm, I love the feeling of lace against my erection. Being turned on all day makes it so much more intense when I come later."

I palm my own cock through the sheets, picturing Beck's expression as he gives into a pleasure he's been riding all day.

"Does that mean I can come over again after

work?"

"I was counting on it." Beck winks at me and then pulls his pants on. "You don't have to rush out or anything. Help yourself to coffee or whatever you find in the kitchen, and you can use the key under the doormat to lock up after you leave."

"Okay. Can I take you out to dinner tonight?"

Beck's eyebrows arch in surprise, but he nods his consent.

"Shit, I'm running late. I'll see you tonight."

Beck

My stomach is in knots as I rush into the office, still unsure what I'm going to say to the partners or my father for that matter. I'm not a miracle worker; I can't wave a magic wand and make the sexual harassment not have happened. I know what they want to hear is that I'm using scare tactics to convince the wronged employee to drop the case all together. But I can't. It's wrong the way he was treated, plain and simple. And maybe Bri was right after all. This isn't the life I want.

I thought being a lawyer meant I would get to help people, not defend greedy, asshole corporations.

"The meeting with the partners was rescheduled for noon," my secretary lets me know as soon as I enter my office.

Great, now I have all morning to obsess over it.

I sink into my large leather chair behind my ostentatious desk and let my mind wander back to the day we spent at Rainbow House. Those kids need me. And the kids in my dance class might not need me in the same way, but they appreciate my time. I'd like to think I make their days and lives just a little brighter.

But here, in this office prison, in these clothes that are anything but me, I'm not doing anyone any good.

Standing outside the conference room where I'm set to meet with the partners feels quite a lot like I'm facing down the firing squad. I'd give anything for my shit kicking heels right now.

With a deep breath I pull back my shoulders and lift my head and then push through the fancy double doors.

I'm met with the gaze of five different sets of eyes. A majority of the expressions range from bored to mildly annoyed, with the exception of my father, who's throwing venomous warning looks in my direction. His eyes scream *don't embarrass me.*

"Have a seat, Becket." Rob Bryson indicates an open seat.

"I have a feeling standing will be more prudent."

My father's eyebrows jump up and his jaw ticks. "All we need to hear is that you resolved the McCullum case in a satisfactory way. Then we can all get back to our day."

"Satisfactory to who?" I challenge.

My father lets out a long-suffering sigh, and the rest of the partners shift uncomfortably. I feel for them; they don't have anything to do with this family drama.

"Is there a problem?" Rich Kramer asks.

"Yeah, Rich, there is a problem." I take another deep breath and look at each of them for a moment. "I don't belong here. That employee was not only sexually harassed, he *was* discriminated against. Unfortunately, the law hasn't caught up to the times. I went to law school to please my father, but also because I want to help people, and that's exactly what I'm going to do."

"Becket," my father barks in a threatening tone.

"No, Father, I'm finished here. *We're* finished."

I turn on my heel and march back to my office to draft my resignation letter.

Gage

My palms are sweating as I pull up in front of Beck's apartment to pick him up for dinner. To my delight, he's still wearing his work clothes. Not that I'm partial to Beck in a suit, but my dick is all for the idea of stripping away the conservative clothes to reveal the real Beck underneath.

"You didn't have to come down to meet me. I was going to come up all gentlemanly."

"I was out walking around a bit so it's not a big deal."

"Is everything okay?" I ask, noticing the strain in his tone.

"Yeah, I handed in my letter of resignation today."

"Holy shit. Is this a celebration dinner then or am I trying to cheer you up?"

Beck laughs and reaches over to put his hand on my thigh. "A little bit of both? I feel a lot lighter and like I'm definitely *going* to be happy. But right now, I feel a little like I failed at fitting in."

"Of course, you failed at fitting in; you were born to stand out, and there's absolutely no shame in that."

His hand on my thigh gives a thankful squeeze and we ride in silence the rest of the way to dinner.

When we get back to Beck's apartment after dinner, all I can think about is stripping him out of that suit and getting my hands and mouth all over him.

"I've been thinking about you and your sexy as fuck lace panties all day."

"Show me?"

I drop to my knees and wrench Beck's pants open. My mouth is already watering for the cock I've been picturing all day.

The outline of his slender, mouthwatering arousal presses against the lace, the shape of his erection stretching the fabric.

Beck's fingers tangle in my hair like he's anchoring himself to me as my hands run along the silky thigh highs exposed now that his pants are around his ankles. It manages to be both arousing and a little sad to know Beck hides his true self beneath the fancy clothes and boring job. I'm glad he quit, even if I won't tell him so. Beck deserves all the happiness he can possibly have.

I shove away those musings and drag my tongue along Beck's lace covered cock, just managing to taste his musk through the fabric and eliciting a shudder and a gasp.

"Fuck, Gage, I've been so hard for you all day."

I groan at his words. The image forms of Beck behind some big fancy desk palming his hard cock through his pants, desperate to come down my throat.

I continue to mouth him through the rough material while reaching around with my free hand and slipping my fingers beneath the panties to tease the cleft of Beck's ass.

He tugs my hair and cants his hips as his panties grow damp with a combination of my saliva and his own pre-cum.

I flick my tongue along the groove where his head meets the shaft and tease my middle finger along the rim of his hole.

"Please," Beck gasps.

My cock pulses, and I moan around a mouthful of his cock.

"Would you fuck me?" I ask, imagining Beck behind me, filling me with his gorgeous cock until I lose my mind.

"Oh god, fuck yes," Beck gasps out between panting breaths. "Let's go to the bedroom where there's condoms and lube."

I haul myself to my feet, and we race for his bedroom. As soon as we're there, I strip while Beck grabs the supplies from his nightstand.

"Can you leave the panties on?" I ask when he starts to remove them.

Beck gives me a dirty smirk and pushes just the front of the panties down, tucking the waist under his balls so his gorgeous cock is free.

As much as I want to look Beck in the eyes while he's inside me, something inside tells me it would be too much this time. I get on my hands and knees, knowing this position will be easier to take both physically and emotionally.

I jump when Beck's fingers, cold with lube, gently trail from my sac to my hole.

"It's okay; I won't hurt you," Beck whispers, his breath tickling just behind my ear. "I only want to make you feel amazing. I want you to know how good you make me feel when you pound my prostate."

I whimper and press my ass back toward him, feeling empty and needing him to fix it.

The tip of one finger slips inside, and I still, waiting to see if this will feel as good as I always imagined.

"Damn, you're tight. You need to try to relax for me, sweetie. You've bottomed before, right?" Beck continues to ease one finger in while using his other hand to stroke my back in a soothing way.

"Um, no, actually."

"Good to know. Try to relax and I promise it'll feel good. If you need me to stop or slow down, let me know."

"I'm not a delicate flower, just get to it." I wiggle my ass encouragingly.

At first, his finger just feels a little weird, not good or bad. Then he crooks it ever so slightly and electric heat explodes in the pit of my stomach and through my balls.

"Holy fuck."

"Gage, meet your prostate."

"Jesus, please just fuck me."

"I need to make sure you're ready," Beck argues.

"I don't want to wait. I don't care if it hurts a little; I want it to."

Beck pulls his finger out, and I hear the condom wrapper tear open.

"Are you sure this is what you want?" Beck's question is punctuated by the pressure of something much larger than a finger against my entrance.

"Yes, fuck yes."

I tense as he pushes in, stretching my tight muscles.

My breath catches at the burn of invasion. I squeeze my eyes closed as my fists clench in the sheets, and my body protests.

"It's okay, sweetie." Beck's lips brush along my shoulders and spine as he holds perfectly still inside me. "Just breathe for me and try to relax."

I take a deep breath and focus on unclenching. Beck's hands continue to caress and soothe. When I manage to relax, Beck slowly eases in a little more and the burning ache returns. This time it's more expected, so I keep taking deep breaths and focusing on the jolt of pleasure I'd gotten from his finger.

It takes a few minutes of slow progress before I feel Beck's thighs flush against mine, the lace from his panties brushing against my ass cheeks, and his cock deep inside me.

I turn my head toward the full-length mirror hanging from Beck's closet door and catch the image of Beck, powerful and beautiful behind me, my own throbbing cock dangling between my legs, aching for release.

"Fuck me, please," I growl, needing to feel him moving deep inside me.

Beck chuckles and leans close to my ear, his breath bathing the back of my neck. "Don't be a bossy bottom. I'm in charge tonight, and you're going to shut up and take it."

He punctuates his sentence by pulling out slowly and then slamming back in, dragging a deep groan from the pit of my stomach. I fall forward on my arms so my ass is high in the air, completely at Beck's mercy.

"That's more like it," Beck praises, finding a steady, hard rhythm with his thrusts.

I spread my knees a little farther apart, and Beck groans as he sinks deeper. I drag in ragged breaths, my nerve endings firing with each thrust of Beck's long cock.

Beck's hands roam over my ass cheeks and hips as he fucks me, muttering incoherent praise. When the broad head of his cock glides over that spot deep inside me he found with his finger earlier, I let out a strangled cry.

"Oh god, right there."

Beck groans as he pounds me harder, sending electric shocks through me and hitting that magic spot over and over, driving me toward orgasm quicker than I'd planned.

I fist the sheets and turn my head again so I can watch as Beck fucks the cum out of me. The sight of his lace panties bunched low on his ass sends a shiver down my spine. I don't give a fuck how feminine Beck dresses, he's a hell of a top.

Beck turns his gaze toward the mirror, and

our eyes lock. He gives me a lazy smirk as he leans forward, his hard pace never stuttering, and whispers in my ear.

"Look how fucking hot you look taking my cock. Now be a good boy and cum for me."

I moan, deep from my core, as my balls draw up tight, and a pulse of hard pleasure punches me in the gut. I roll my hips against his thrusts, chasing the throbbing heat as it unfurls inside me, sending me hurtling into pleasure.

Beck fucks me through my orgasm as my cum splashes all over his sheets. And just as my legs start to quake, unable to hold my weight any longer, he clutches my shoulder tight and cries out, throwing his head back. I marvel at the feel of his cock pulsing out his pleasure deep inside me, part of me wishing I could feel the heat of his cum filling me.

When my legs finally give way, Beck collapses on top of me with an exhausted laugh.

"Damn."

"Yeah," I agree.

After a few minutes, Beck gets up and cleans himself up and then comes back to bed where I haven't had the strength to move yet.

When he climbs in beside me, I roll toward him, wrapping my arms around him and pulling him against my sweaty chest.

"So, what made you want to bottom for me if you haven't before?"

"I've always wanted to, but with Johnny, it

just never happened. We were young and didn't experiment with too much, just sort of stuck with the *assumed* roles. And I wasn't about to bottom for one of the few random guys I picked up since then."

"Was Johnny your first?"

"No, but no one special came before him. I guess I was waiting for the right person."

Beck is quiet for a long time as I run my fingers through his hair.

"Thank you for sharing yourself with me. Thank you for trusting me," he says after his long silence. "I hope it was good."

"Fuck yeah, that was incredible. I prefer topping, but definitely something I'd be up for every so often."

Once my words are out, I realize how they sound: like we're in a long-term relationship. It sounds like I expect Beck to be the man I'm sharing my bed with for months or years in the future. The scariest part is the implication doesn't feel wrong.

Beck chuckles. "Works for me, sweetie. You know I'm a greedy bottom."

I chuckle and move my hand down to his ass to grab a handful.

"Hmm, you're fucking hot is what you are."

CHAPTER 21

Gage

Beck frets in front of the mirror, putting on, and then removing, several shades of eye shadow before I come up behind him and plant a kiss on the back of his neck.

"You look sexy as fuck, no matter what you wear. And Adam and Nox already love you, so you don't need to worry."

"They've only met me twice briefly, how can they love me?" Beck argues.

Because you've made me smile again. Because you brought sunshine back into my life. Because I can't explain what I'm feeling toward you, but whatever it is, Adam can tell, and he loves you for it.

"Because they're good judges of character."

Beck rolls his eyes and starts to apply a shimmery rainbow color to his eyelids. "Can you grab me a pair of black thigh highs and my black lace panties?"

Heat flares in the pit of my stomach. "You're just mean if you expect me to spend the whole night in front of my friends with a raging hard on."

"Aw, poor baby," Beck mocks with a smirk. "I promise to take good care of you when we get home tonight."

It doesn't escape my attention that he referred to his apartment as *home*, nor does the air of comfort and familiarity. But I don't mention it. I don't know how to deal with my heart expanding in my chest. For so long, there was nothing more than an empty space inside my rib cage where my heart used to be. Now, my heart is too big and too full to handle.

I go to Beck's dresser and grab the requested items, my cock immediately responding to the feel of lace under my fingertips.

I hand them over, and Beck puts the finishing touches on his makeup before standing and shrugging out of his silky pink robe. His own cock is semi-hard. He gives me a sultry wink when he notices me staring.

Over his thigh highs and lace he tugs on a pair of jeans, and a shiver runs down my spine. I love being the only one who knows what he's hiding under his clothes. Not that I ever want Beck to hide, but I do love unwrapping him at the end of the night.

"Ready to go?" I ask once he's pulled on a shirt and slipped into a pair of black pumps.

"Ready as I'll ever be."

"Holy balls, this is my jam," Beck declares, shoving his beer toward me. "Hold my beer, I need to get my groove on."

I watch in barely concealed amusement as Beck jumps up from the table and starts dancing to *Single Ladies*, no doubt hitting every one of Beyoncé's moves with precision. It only takes a few seconds for two girls from a nearby table to join him, their boyfriends looking less than impressed with the turn of events.

"I can't remember when I've seen you this happy," Adam says.

I search my memory and come up blank. "I can't remember the last time I *was* this happy. Beck is..." I don't even have words to describe how he makes me feel.

He's laughing and giving pointers to the girls who've joined him, but his own grace, in a pair of high heels no less, never falters.

Beck catches my eye and winks at me as he mouths the words with a saucy smile, something about putting a ring on it, and for some reason, my heart flutters in my chest.

When the song ends, he gives both the women a hug and then returns to our table with a smile.

"Sorry, sometimes the music moves me," Beck apologizes to Nox and Adam.

"Don't be sorry, just teach me how to move like that," Nox says, eyeing Beck with admiration.

"I do teach dance, and I'm always happy to

give free lessons to friends," Beck tells Nox and then turns to Adam. "I'd be happy to teach your man some pole dancing moves too in exchange for dirt on Gage."

Adam throws his head back and laughs. "Deal."

"I'm beginning to see this was a mistake," I deadpan.

"Shut up; I'm making your friends love me." Beck elbows me in the ribs, and I playfully grab his arm and yank him closer, claiming his lips in a quick kiss.

When I release him, I see a shocked smile on Adam's face.

This is what living feels like.

"You'll spend the night, right?" Beck asks as he leads me up to his apartment.

I didn't expect sleeping at Beck's to become so routine, but over the past week, I've slept here four nights. And the nights I spent at home were fucking torture.

"Yeah, I'll stay," I agree.

Threading my fingers through Beck's hair, I angle his face so I can claim his lips.

With the unfamiliar warmth still prickling just under the surface of my skin, this kiss isn't like any of the previous ones we've shared. It's not frenzied or delicious in its filth. This is a slow, sweet coupling that steals my breath as our lips dance and taste in tandem like we have all the time in the world. The intensity of the emotions it brings to the surface threaten to suffocate me, but I can't pull away.

Minutes or hours later, when we finally manage to part, I feel a small shiver ripple through Beck's body. He looks up at me, his eyes filled with questions I don't have answers to.

"Let's go to bed," he suggests in a husky tone before reaching between us and knotting our fingers together.

I can only manage to nod, my thoughts and emotions too jumbled to form words as I let him lead me to his bedroom.

Beck strips his shirt and jeans off, leaving him looking mouthwatering in his black thigh high stockings and black lace panties. Then, he climbs onto the bed and lays on his back to wait for me.

I shed my clothes as well and crawl onto the bed, hovering over him. Still in the mood to tease and savor, I bury my nose against his neck and inhale, filling my lungs with his unique, sweet, yet musky scent.

My stomach flutters and my cock throbs, my body immediately associating the feel of Beck's smooth skin against mine and his essence surrounding me as a clear sign of forthcoming pleasure.

I trail my lips down the column of Beck's throat, nipping at his collarbone as I pass. He gasps and squirms against me, his arousal pressing against my hip through his panties.

I continue my journey down his chest and over the grooves of his toned stomach.

I can't resist the tease of running my tongue along the edge of his panties when I reach them. When I ghost my mouth over the outline of his cock through the lace, Beck curses and claws at my hair.

I take my time peeling off his stockings one at a time before returning to his panties. By the time I loop my fingers through the waist and tug them off, they're already damp with pre-cum.

His erection bobs free, and my mouth waters. But instead of devouring him like I'm dying to do, I place a chaste kiss at the base of his cock and then pat his thigh.

"Flip over."

Beck obeys, readily rolling onto his stomach.

I trace my finger along the curve of his ass and then gently kiss the intricate pattern tattooed on his skin from the lace.

I give his back the same treatment the front received, kissing and touching every plane and valley, memorizing him inch by inch.

Once I'm satisfied, I part the perky globes of his ass and tease my tongue from his taint to his pucker.

"Oh fuck," Beck gasps, his hips thrusting against the bed. "Please, baby, I need you inside me."

Baby. Of all the pet names he uses, that's my favorite. I haven't heard him call others *baby*. It feels special, like I'm something different to him than anyone else.

I reach for the bottle of lube and a condom from the nightstand.

Once my fingers are generously coated, I slip them into the cleft of Beck's ass. He lets out a little sigh as I press one finger inside his hot, tight hole.

I'm barely one knuckle deep when Beck starts pushing back against my hand, pulling me deeper.

"More."

He groans as I add a second finger and start to fuck him, making sure the pads of my fingers graze his prostate with each pass.

"More," he cries again.

I reach for the condom and tear it open with my teeth before quickly sheathing myself.

When I pull my fingers free, Beck raises to his hands and knees, but I need more. I need to see his eyes as I push inside him.

I grab Beck's hips and flip him over again so he's on his back. And then I position myself between his legs, our eyes locked as I press into him.

A deep groan tears from my throat as I breach the tight ring of muscle.

"Yes," Beck gasps, his fingers biting into my

shoulder blades as his body arches against mine as though he's subconsciously trying to ensure as many points of contact as possible.

The low-level warmth, which has been blossoming under my skin since the bar earlier tonight, explodes into a raging inferno, threatening to raze me to ashes.

I can't tear my gaze from Beck's as his pupils dilate, and his eyes cloud with pleasure.

I set a slow, steady pace, dragging my heavy cock over his swollen prostate.

"Oh Jesus, Gage," Beck gasps, throwing his head back and biting down on his bottom lip.

"You're so gorgeous, so perfect. Beck, I—" I bite down on my tongue to stop the words from tumbling free. I bury my face in the crook of his neck and wrap him in my arms, holding him against me as I continue to claim him, ravage him, *own* him.

"I'm coming," Beck cries out.

Wet heat coats my stomach as his cock pulses between us. His tight channel clamps down around me, dragging my own pleasure out of me. I gasp and moan against Beck's sweet skin as waves of ecstasy crash over me. As I come down from the high, I realize I'm clutching Beck to my chest like my life depends on it.

When I finally manage to release him, he shivers before collapsing against the pillow with a sleepy, sated smile.

Liam's words from a few weeks ago echo in

my mind *That sounds like love.*

Could it be love? Is it possible that I've fallen in love with Beck?

I glance down at a now sleeping Beck, nestled in my arms with a content smile on his lips, and my whole body fills with an inexplicable fullness and warmth.

It's different than how I felt about Johnny, but no less intense or important. Does it feel the same every time you love someone different? Cas said it's different, and that made sense. He was right; *I'm* not the same, so how can my feelings be?

Beck makes a sleepy sound and nuzzles closer, and my heart feels *too* full, tears prickling behind my eyes. Not sad tears, more like I'm feeling too much and need to release it in some way.

I ghost my fingertips along the smooth skin of Beck's cheek, and then I lean in to brush a kiss to his forehead.

I feel like I've been waiting for Beck for years without ever realizing it. But I think he came into my life at exactly the right time. I wasn't ready before now to consider letting anyone in. It's like Beck knew I was ready to live again, and he appeared like a guardian angel to teach me how. He's light and life. He's everything, and I can't imagine ever letting him go.

Beck sleeps soundly in my arms, all the while a storm is raging inside me.

I want to pull him tighter against me and simultaneously shove him away.

It's all too much, too good, too full, too danger-ous to risk losing everything.

My heart thunders like I'm a trapped ani-mal, and all I can think about is getting space and air to breathe.

I ease out of bed, careful not to disturb Beck. I don't bother to get dressed because even in a state of emotional turmoil, I can't convince my-self that I should leave in the middle of the night. Beck's hold on me is too strong and that's the whole problem.

I sit down on the couch in the living room and bury my face in my hands. I force myself to count my breaths as I try to calm down so I can think clearly.

I loved Johnny with everything inside me. But, somehow, what I feel for Beck is bigger and fuller than anything I've felt before. It feels like an utter betrayal to think such a thing.

Something wet nudges my arm, startling me out of my downward spiral. I pull my hands from my face and look over to see Frodo, Beck's antisocial cat staring at me, pressing his nose to various spots on my arm.

"Hey buddy." I move my hand slowly to-ward him, and he glowers at me. After a few sec-onds, he lets out a little huff and headbutts my hand. "I know how you feel. You want someone to pet and love you, but you miss your person." Frodo lets out a little meow of what I can only as-sume is agreement. "Maybe it's okay to have a new person now? Maybe you can keep your old person in your heart and make room for a new one too? Beck is a great person, you'd be lucky to have his love. We both would."

Frodo meows again and curls up beside me, pressed against my thigh. I slowly stroke his fur and think about life and love and the meaning of it all.

CHAPTER 22

Gage

October seventeenth, ten years to the day that Johnny left, taking all the best parts of me with him...or at least that's what I've always thought. If you'd have asked me a few months ago, I would've told you there was absolutely no way I could feel anything again. I was numb and that's the way I liked it. Numb was the only way I could cope with the loss of my whole heart and soul.

Except my heart and soul may not be gone.

Gorgeous Beck, so full of life and unable to abandon me in my sorrow.

He refused to leave me alone when I tried to brush him off, and now he's reawakened me body and spirit.

But what does it all mean? And how can I even be thinking about Beck on the anniversary of Johnny's death?

I pull up in front of Adam's parents' house and get out of the car with a bouquet of wild-flowers clutched tightly in my fist. Twice a year, I bring Johnny flowers to the gazebo where I first told him I loved him on his seventeenth birthday. It was only a few months before I lost him forever.

I was so young and stupid. I thought we had forever together, but I didn't know how long forever
really was.

I go around the side of the house without
bothering to go say hi to Mr. and Mrs. Truman.
They're like I was a few months ago, shells of their
former selves, only going through the motions of
living.

The gazebo is the same as always as I step inside and set the flowers down on the bench. Then
I lean against one wall and close my eyes, letting
the heavy presence of memories of joy and agony
wash over me.

"Ten years, Jay. Ten years I've been without you. You know what really scares me?" I ask
no one. "I'm terrified of reaching the year where
you'll have been gone longer than you were ever
here. And I'm afraid of letting you go. But I'm also
afraid of not grabbing on to the feelings Beck is
stirring in me and letting myself live again. I guess
I'm afraid of a lot, huh?" I laugh at myself and wipe
a few stray tears from my cheeks. "I still don't
understand how you could've left us like you did,
Jay. Adam is doing well, though, so that's a bright
spot at least."

I stand and stretch my arms over my head
and then put them against the wall, dropping my
head between my shoulders.

"I think some of the numbness I cloaked myself in was to avoid how angry I was. I was so mad
at you, Jay. I was mad at myself, too. How could

I have let you down like that? Beck says it wasn't my fault. I want to believe him. I want to be able to forgive myself and move forward. I don't want to keep feeling like I was cheated out of a life because my stupid heart fell too hard in love with a man who was too short in this world."

A sob wracks through my chest, and I suck in a deep breath as the tears fall unrestrained.

"I'm sorry I couldn't have done better by you, Jay. I need to know if it's okay for me to move on, or if the guilt and suffocating loneliness are meant to be my penance for letting you down."

Later, when I'm driving home, I get a call from Adam.

"Hello?" I answer, my raspy voice betraying that I've been crying for the past hour.

"You on your way over?"

"Yeah, I'll be there in a few minutes," I assure him.

"Okay, see you soon, man."

My raging sorrow has simmered into a quiet melancholy by the time I pull up to my old apartment.

As soon as I'm through the door, Adam has his arms around me, hugging me fiercely.

"I'm okay," I whisper but I let his hold comfort me, a fresh wave of tears building behind my eyes.

"I know you are." Adam pats my back and then releases me. "Come on, I ordered take-out, and Nox is having a slumber party at Dani's, so it's just the two of us, like old times."

"Sounds great."

We settle onto the couch with containers of my favorite Indian place on the coffee table in front of us, and Adam flips on an episode of *Tattoo Nightmares*.

"There's a Halloween party at Rainbow House. I know you don't usually come, but I thought maybe..."

A little bit of the heaviness in my heart lifts as I try to imagine what kind of costume Beck would wear to a party at Rainbow House. I'm sure he'd be thrilled to go.

"Let me talk to Beck and see if he has plans yet," I hedge, knowing he'll be dying to go but I may chicken out of asking him.

Adam's smile is filled with so much more than just happiness over a party. I know he sees it as symbolic and is reading a lot into my tentative agreement. Maybe it *is* symbolic.

Beck

I'm sitting on my couch lazily stroking Frodo, who inexplicably is all for being pet, when my phone starts to ring.

I jump to answer it, hoping like hell it's Gage. He told me last week that this was the anniversary of Johnny's death and that he'd need a day or so to cope; I shouldn't worry if I didn't hear from him. But I've hoped like hell all day I'd hear from him. I want to be there for him to ease his pain.

I see Gage's name across my screen, and some of the tension eases from my chest.

"Hey, baby."

"Hi." Gage's voice is hoarse and strained.

I want to reach through the phone and soothe a hand over his face and along his back. I want to pull Gage against me and hold him while he cries out all his sorrows. And then I want to kiss him until he smiles again.

I want to tell him I thought about him all day and that I fucking love him. Luckily, my brain filters my mouth before I can blurt that embarrassing admission out.

"Frodo is letting me pet him," I say instead and then cringe over how dumb I sound. Gage is quiet, so I go on, not knowing what else is safe to talk about. "It was so random; he just curled up next to me and let out this sad little meow like he was saying, 'I get that she's not coming back, and I'm lonely'. Then I started to rub the top of his head, and he made this happy little cooing noise...so I guess we're bros now or something."

There's a sound from Gage's end of the phone that sounds like a mix between a laugh and a sob.

"You seem to have a talent for that," Gage

finally says.

"What's that?"

"Helping heartbroken creatures and re-minding them they can be loved again."

My heart stills at that word, *love*. Does Gage know how gone I am over him?

"Gage, I—"

"Do you want to go to a Halloween party at Rainbow House in a few weeks?"

My brain stutters over the question for a few seconds, trying to make sense of the non-sequitur.

"Um, yeah, that sounds awesome."

"Great."

"Great," I echo in a bit of a daze.

"I had a long day, so I'm going to go to sleep. I just wanted to hear your voice first."

"Oh...okay. Night."

"Night."

CHAPTER 23

Gage

Beck's cheeks sparkle with glitter, and his eyes dance with amusement as I try to pull on the tights he insisted "brought the costume together".

"I can't believe I let you talk me into this."

"Excuse me, but *you* invited *me* to this party," Beck corrects as he stands up and smoothes his short green dress.

"Yeah, but I didn't want to wear tights. Why don't you have to wear tights?" I gripe, but it's halfhearted because I'm having a hard time tearing my eyes away from Beck's smooth, long legs.

"Because Peter Pan wears tights, Tinker Bell doesn't."

Beck shrugs into a pair of wings and then checks himself over in his full-length mirror.

I finally get the tights up, but my junk is all squished, and somehow, I also have a wedgie.

"Here, let me help," Beck says with a chuckle.

He reaches into my tights and rearranges my cock and balls without batting an eye, causing blood to rush south and making the whole situation more difficult.

"Tights and erections don't go well to-gether."

"No, they don't," Beck agrees with a laugh. "There you go."

He finishes fixing my tights and then gives me a playful pat on the ass.

"I can't remember the last time I dressed up for Halloween," I muse.

"That's crazy. I dress up every year. Hallow-een is my favorite. Just remind me not to bend over though. This dress is too short, and I don't want to end up mooning children."

I can't resist reaching out to trail a finger along his upper thigh, just below the hem of his dress.

"You make a cute fairy," I tease.

"I know." Beck smirks and then pops up on his toes to press his lips firmly against mine. "Now, let's go have some fun."

I tug self-consciously at my outfit as we enter Rainbow House and draw the gaze of all my friends.

"You made it!" Royal shouts from across the room.

I chuckle at the sight of Royal, Zade, Nash, and Liam all covered in green body paint and vari-ous color bandanas.

"Are you guys the Ninja Turtles?" I guess, and Zade whips out a pair of nunchucks in response.

"You're hilarious."

"Sure, we're hilarious now. You should've been there as I tried to convince these dumbasses that they couldn't go to a Halloween party for teenagers dressed as pornstars," Nash gripes about his boyfriends, but the love in his eyes gives him away.

"Wait, how do porn stars dress?" I ask in confusion.

"Exactly," Nash says drolly and everyone laughs.

Without thought I reach for Beck's hand, and we make our way around the party to greet everyone.

Adam and Nox are dressed as Batman and Robin. Dani is a mermaid with some seriously killer makeup that looks like shimmering scales around her eyes that Beck grills her about how to achieve. Owen seems to have joined up with Royal's crew and is dressed as a rat in a karate uniform, otherwise known as Splinter. I pause when we reach Madden and Thane.

"I don't get it." I look back and forth between their odd and creepy costumes.

"Pennywise and The Babadook, hottest gay couple around right now, duh."

"Ooookay."

Beck and I share a laugh. I can't get over how

much fun I'm having and we just barely got here.

I glance over at Beck, and my heart constricts. He looks so pretty and happy. I wish I could bottle his essence and keep it with me always.

Kyle approaches us dressed as Lady Gaga. Beck spends the next few minutes gushing over what a great job Kyle did on his makeup and then suggesting a few Gaga dance moves.

"Having fun?" Adam asks.

"Yeah, surprisingly, I am."

"It looks good on you."

"Thanks." I bite my lip against the emotion that threatens to spill over. Is it wrong to feel happy and have fun two weeks after the anniversary of Johnny's death?

"It's been long enough; it's time for you to be happy," Adam says as if reading my mind.

"It's time to Monster Mash," Beck declares, dragging me into a throng of teenagers and we all start jumping around in time to the music.

Beck

I laugh and jump and drink in all the energy in the room.

Every time I spot a kid not joining in, I scurry over to pull them into the fray, making it my personal mission to ensure everyone is having the best Halloween ever.

"I need something to drink," Gage calls over the loud din, and I follow him out of the mass of thrashing teens and adults acting like teens.

Instead of heading for the punch bowl, Gage takes my hand and veers for the sliding door that leads to the backyard.

"What are we—" My question is cut off by Gage's lips attacking mine as he shoves me up against the side of the building.

I moan into his mouth as our tongues tangle. I laugh against his lips as my dress starts to tent, and I grind against him.

"Mmm, I'm so glad you aren't wearing tights, much easier access." Gage trails his fingers up my inner thigh and then cups my balls through my panties. I groan quietly, hyper-aware of the fact that there's a room full of teenagers a few feet away.

Our hands fumble frantically, our lips and teeth clashing together as we get lost in each other.

"Oh, shit," a startled voice has Gage and I jumping apart.

I tug at the hem of my dress to hide my erection and catch Gage doing the same.

"What are you doing out here?" Gage asks, eyeing Liam and Kyle suspiciously once he gets his head on straight again.

"Um..." Liam glances at Kyle like he's trying to figure out how to answer. Kyle just shrugs and gives us a sheepish smile. "We came out to look at the stars."

"Suuuure you did," Gage says with a put-upon sigh. "I doubt you want Royal catching you guys *looking at the stars*, so I'd suggest you save it for another night when odds aren't at least even that he'll be out here soon to fool around with Nash, Zade, or both."

"Good call," Liam nods in agreement before spinning around and tugging Kyle back toward the building.

As soon as they're gone, Gage and I burst out laughing. The sexy moment is over, but damn if it doesn't feel incredible to have Gage sagging against me in a fit of giggles.

"I'm glad we came tonight," Gage says when he catches his breath.

"Me too."

CHAPTER 24

Gage

"If this isn't your thing, then I'm just about out of ideas," Beck warns as we climb out of the car at the state park he chose for a hiking adventure.

Beck looks cute as fuck in what he deemed his hiking outfit. He's wearing relaxed fit jeans and a pair of hiking boots he bought last week and has spent days breaking in. For his top he chose a pink, sparkly flannel shirt. Honest to god, I have no idea where he found such a thing, but everything about him makes me want to tackle him to the ground and kiss the hell out of him.

Beck holds up a hand to cover his eyes from getting too much sun, and then he looks over at me with a hopeful smile.

"We're going to have fun today," he says with confidence.

It hits me that Beck has been on this mission to remind me how to have fun for two months now. Even though I haven't found an exact activity that really gets me excited, I can say without a doubt that spending time with Beck is *always* fun. He's reminded me how to laugh and smile. He's reminded me what physical pleasure feels like and why getting out of bed every day is worth it. He's changed me and saved me. There's no doubt in my mind I'm falling for him, or possibly have already fallen. The night I spent sitting on his couch with Frodo didn't produce answers about what I should do about my feelings. But maybe I've taken steps to accepting that it must be possible to have loved Johnny and still love Beck now.

We don't waste time finding the trail and heading into the woods. I take a deep breath, letting the cool morning air fill my lungs.

Neither of us bother with conversation. Instead, content to bathe in the sounds of birds and wind and possibly a far-off river. Twigs and leaves crunch under our feet, and the occasional chipmunk scampers across the path up ahead.

"Okay, *this* I like," I admit as we stop on a bluff and look out over vast treetops. "It's so peaceful."

"Yay, I win," Beck crows with pride.

"Yeah, you did. You beat my grumpy ass into fun submission."

"Happy to be of service." Beck reaches for my hand, and then his expression turns a little sad. "You're about ready to leave the nest, little birdy. Your wing is just about healed."

"What?"

"Nothing, don't mind me," Beck laughs, but his eyes are still full of sorrow.

"Let's keep going."

Beck

I know I'm too quiet on the drive back to town after our hike. I can feel Gage glancing in my direction every few moments, worried about my sudden turn to melancholy.

I promised myself I'd let him go once my work was done, but my heart hurts at the thought. Maybe I can keep him as a friend. I can give myself one last night of *more* and then tomorrow tell him we should just be friends from now on.

"Do you want to come to my place?" Gage asks abruptly.

My breath catches in my throat. Gage has never invited me over. He's never hinted he wanted to open that part of his life to me.

"Sounds good," I agree.

Maybe Gage is on the same wavelength, planning for this to be our last night together and wanting it to be a sweet goodbye. That's exactly what I'd already decided on, so why does it make me feel so sick to think Gage agrees?

It's not long before Gage is leading me up to his apartment, a third-floor walkup with a decent view of the city.

"This is a nice place."

Gage snorts a laugh. "It's not warm or homey like your place. That's why I haven't had you over, I figured you'd think this place was too cold or something."

"Aw, baby, I don't think that. But if you want

to decorate, I'd be happy to help you figure out your style," I offer, grasping for another project to help Gage with. That doesn't mean we can keep hooking up. But maybe helping him decorate his apartment can signify the start of our platonic friendship.

"I could really use a shower after that hike. Care to join me?"

"I'm too tired to move," I complain.

Gage chuckles and gives me a kiss on the side of the head. It's almost too much for my heart to take in this moment.

"Why don't you go get in bed, and I'll meet you in there in a minute," Gage's hot breath tickles my ear and sends a shiver down my spine.

"Don't keep me waiting too long."

A warm satisfaction settles over me as I step into Gage's bedroom for the first time. I'd be willing to bet I'm the only man who's been in his bedroom in nine years. Looking around, I notice the tan and light blue color scheme is warm and welcoming, but it's certainly less chaotic than my own room.

Deciding I want to make Gage work for it a little bit, I leave my clothes on as I climb onto his bed.

As soon as I'm settled against his pillow, a framed photo on the nightstand catches my eye.

I roll toward it and notice it's a picture of a young-looking Gage, his hair a sandy color and the haunted look absent from his eyes. Beside him is an even younger looking man who I can only assume is Johnny based on the way Gage has his arms around him. They seem to be enjoying a day at the beach. But what really grabs my attention is that Johnny is wearing makeup.

Relief and disappointment war in my chest as I contemplate what this means. Either he's really into guys wearing makeup, in which case, yay for me. Or, I'm nothing more than a stand-in for the man he lost.

I set the photo back down seconds before Gage comes in with a wolfish grin and a towel around his waist.

"You're wearing too many clothes," he comments, crawling onto the bed. By the time he's hovering over me, he notices I'm not on the same page.

"What's wrong?"

"Nothing," I force a smile, willing the uncomfortable feeling in my gut to subside.

Gage's smile falters, and then he glances over at the picture, slightly askew on the nightstand, and understanding dawns in his eyes.

"It's weird that I've got a picture of Johnny by my bed, isn't it?"

"No," I rush to assure him. "I'm sorry I'm being weird. We're fuck buddies; what do I care whose picture you have by your bed?"

"What if we were more than fuck buddies?"

"Oh, sugar, please don't go there. The last thing I'm about to do is compete with a ghost.

This is fun. Can't it just be fun?"

"Beck," Gage reaches for me with a heart-breaking expression on his face. It's like I'm ripping his heart out. But that can't be true because I never had his heart to begin with. "I lo-"

"I'm kind of tired; I think I'm just going to go home. Raincheck?" I force a smile and scoot off the bed.

Gage's face goes a little pale, and I notice a hitch in his breathing. And then it hits me what a trigger this is for him, me leaving on possibly bad terms.

I reach for him and cup his jaw so he's looking at me. I run my thumb along the slight stubble on his jaw

"This isn't a fight. This is a much-needed re-evaluation. It would probably be good for you to re-evaluate, too. As hard as I tried not to get my heart involved, I'm afraid I might have failed. I'm not so sure I can do casual anymore, but I'm also very serious when I tell you I can't spend my life competing with a ghost. I'm afraid we may be at an impasse. Take some time to think, and don't worry about me, I'm safe and generally happy. This is *not* the last time you'll see me."

Gage let's out a shaky breath and then nods before wrapping his arms around my middle in a tight hug. When he releases me, neither of us seems to know what else to say, so without another word, I turn and leave Gage's apartment, leaving my heart behind.

Gage

I watch wordlessly as Beck flees from my apartment like it's on fire. My chest aches, and my heart feels like the tentatively placed pieces could fall apart again at any second.

How could he leave like that?

I look at the picture of Johnny on my nightstand and try to see it with new eyes. Is it creepy or weird that I still have it there?

I'd been about to tell Beck that I wanted things to be real between us. But if things were real, if Beck was my *boyfriend,* would that make it wrong to have a picture of Johnny?

I lay the framed photo face down so I don't have to look at it for the moment, and then I crawl into bed and grab for the pillow Beck's head rested against for a few short minutes.

Didn't Beck realize what a big deal it was for me to invite him into my space like this?

Is he right that we need space to figure out what we both want?

CHAPTER 25

Beck

I've reached for my phone a thousand times today to call Gage and make sure he's okay.

I shouldn't have left him like that without more of a conversation, but it was all too much. I couldn't afford the hope of letting myself believe Gage might really want more.

At least there's one bright spot on this day. It's my first day full time at On Point, and then afterward, I'll be going by Rainbow House to talk with Mary about their possible legal needs.

My life is finally being shaped into something I'm truly proud of. I only wish Bri was here to see it. Or that I could call Gage and tell him how excited I am for this new chapter. Or that I could go home at the end of today, cuddle into his arms, and tell him all about it.

"Holy shit, you're on time," Clay teases as I walk through the door of On Point.

"Now I don't have a bullshit job to deal with beforehand," I point out.

"True. I'm so fucking happy you finally quit that soul suck. Tell me you're happy?"

I force a smile. I'm happy I finally told my

father to shove it. But there's still the matter of the missing piece of my heart.

"What's wrong?" Clay picks up on my somber mood immediately.

"Ugh," I groan at the question.

"Oh no, what happened?"

"It's Gage...he wants *more*," I divulge like it's an illness.

Clay fixes me with a disapproving look, pursing his lips and cocking his hip.

"Am I seriously hearing these words right now?"

"Yes. I can't give him more. He almost told me he *loves* me."

"Beck, you are so dumb. How is any of this a bad thing?" Clay frowns at me. "You love him, you idiot."

"He can't love me. He's still in love with his dead boyfriend."

"Sweetcheeks, love is not a finite resource. He can love you and still love the man he lost."

I shake my head at Clay and clench my eyes against all the emotions raging inside me.

"Can we not talk about this right now?"

Clay sighs and gives me a kiss on the cheek. "Fine, but this isn't over. At least one of us should be happy and in love."

"Then you'd better find a way to turn Max over to the D," I counter and Clay bristles.

"Leave it alone."

"I will if you will," I counter.

"Fine," Clay gripes before spinning on his heel and stalking off.

"After my classes this morning I need to go deal with my parents."

Clay eyes my outfit. "Are you stopping home to change and wash off your makeup?"

"Nope," I answer with as much sass as I can manage, which is a hell of a lot of sass. "I'm done with their bullshit. I need to get the key to Bri's storage unit and tell them where they can shove it."

"You want me to come with for moral support?" he offers.

"No thanks, sweets. I'll see you later." I give Clay a quick kiss on the cheek before heading to my studio to prepare for my early class.

Instead of dawdling in my car like I normally do when I get to my parent's house, I'm in full on shit kicking form. I stride to the door and knock forcefully. It only takes a few seconds for the housekeeper to answer it, and when she does, I can see the surprise in her expression when she takes in my outfit.

"Hello, Maria, I'm here to speak to my parents."

"Becket? Are you here to explain that stunt you pulled this week and grovel for your job back?" my dad barks from somewhere inside the house.

"No, I'm here to get the key to Bri's storage unit."

Moments later both of them appear behind Maria.

"I thought you were past this phase," my father drones as he takes in my outfit with barely concealed distaste.

"It was never a phase. However, bending to your will *was* a phase, and that has officially ended. Now, can I please have the key so I can get her stuff. I'll have it out of your way this afternoon." He narrows his eyes at me and then turns and strides away, hopefully to get the key to the storage unit.

"Becket, what's gotten into you? This isn't like you at all," my mother admonishes.

"This is me, Mom. I haven't let either of you see the real me in a very long time. I'm willing to try to work on a relationship on more even footing, where you both respect my choices and person. But if that's not possible, I understand."

My father returns and thrusts a key at me.

"Thank you. If you decide to call me, you know how to reach me."

Gage

"Hey, Dani, what's new with you?"

Dani blinks in surprise, and I feel like a complete asshole. How did I not realize how isolated I'd let myself become? Even the people I consider

239

my friends...no, they're more than friends. The Heathens crew are my family, and I've been so shitty, they're all surprised at the most basic out-reach on my part. It's well past time for things to change.

"I'm fine," she answers cautiously.

"Cool." I rub the back of my neck and dig deep for a way to connect. "I saw you hanging out with Cas and Beau at Nox's birthday party a few months ago; did that go how you'd been hoping?"

Dani's confused expression morphs into a smile, and then she lets out a snort of a laugh.

"Yeah, it was great. It was just a one-time thing, like a life experience I couldn't pass up. Those two don't need my issues getting between them."

I nod and cast around for something to say in response.

"You know, there's something I've been wrestling with; I'd love a sounding board," Dani says, and a warm happiness spreads through me at the gesture.

"Of course, what's up?"

Dani hops onto the stool beside me behind the desk at Heathens and leans closer so she can talk quietly.

"A few months ago, I overheard Madden and Thane talking about kids after they get married. They were discussing adoption versus surrogacy, and it seemed like, while they clearly want to adopt too, they're dying to have a biological child as well. The thing is, I know how expensive surrogacy can be, plus it's not easy to find someone willing to do it. And... well...I'm not really using my uterus for anything useful. Do you think it's crazy for me to consider offering it to them?"

"Wow." The back of my throat aches a little at what an incredible gesture that is. And I can only imagine the joy Madden and Thane will experience at bringing a child into the world together. They'll be great dads. "I think that's an amazing thing to give them."

"I know it's a big decision, which is why I've forced myself to take time to consider all angles of it. But I feel like I really want to do this for them. Would it be tacky or weird to give it to them as a wedding present?"

I chuckle at the image of Dani putting a giant bow on her stomach and telling them the news.

"That's a great idea. Way to make everyone else's toasters and whatever else look like shit."

Dani laughs and then hops off the stool to give me a hug.

"Thank you. I needed confirmation that I wasn't crazy."

"You're definitely crazy, but you're also generous, and you're going to make them so fucking happy."

"That's me, I'm like a fucking fairy, spreading sunshine and glitter and shit."

Pretty sure that's Beck.

"Now, if you'll excuse me, I need to go talk to Adam."

Walking into Adam's office, I can feel the tension radiating off him as he works on one of the spreadsheets he hates so much.

A wave of guilt crashes over me. We always said Heathens would be *ours,* but I've left him holding the bag this whole time because I couldn't pull my head out of my ass and find a way to deal with my grief.

"Hey man, what's up?" Adam asks as I sit in the chair opposite his desk.

"I think I owe you an apology. I've been so entrenched in my own loss for so long, I haven't been a good friend. I ignored the fact that you were dealing with the loss of your brother, and I didn't live up to my promises to you regarding this place."

Adam blinks at me, shock written all over his face.

"I never begrudged you your time to grieve. But I'm not going to lie, it's been good to start seeing glimpses of my old friend again these past few months. Hang on tight to Beck; he's good for you."

I flinch at the mention of Beck. I don't know where things went so wrong last night, but I decided I'm going to give him some space and do soul searching like he suggested. Then I'm going to do what I can to convince him to take a chance on a man who might still have some chips and cracks but is finally in one piece again.

"I want to buy into my half of the business, if you'll have me. I want to take on some of the responsibilities you hate, like crunching numbers. I want to be a full partner in Heathens like we always talked about."

Adam smiles and then holds out his hand. "Give me your wallet."

I cock an eyebrow but don't argue.

Adam opens it and takes out the twenty dollars I have in there and hands me the rest of my wallet back.

"Congratulations, you're now half owner of Heathens Ink. We'll find a lawyer and get the papers drawn up."

I stand and stride around the desk to pull Adam into a tight hug.

"Love you, man."

Adam laughs and pats my back.

"Love you too, dude."

Pulling up to the small beach I visited with Johnny one summer, more than a lifetime ago, is like a punch in the stomach.

Memories of that happy day only a few short months before Johnny was gone play through my mind. I remember picking him up that morning from his house and seeing the joyful smile on his face when I told him we were going to the beach. He was so beautiful and free that day, and I thought it was a turning point in our relationship. It turned out it was, but not in the way I'd hoped. Thinking back, that was one of the last good days we had, Johnny becoming emotional and erratic after that. But I've held the joyful day when we splashed in the ocean and kissed in the sand as a precious jewel clutched close to my fractured heart.

I climb out of my car, leaving my shoes behind so I can feel the sand between my toes, and head down toward the water.

A conversation I had with Johnny that night comes to mind.

"The night sky makes me think of you now, did you know that?" Johnny said and even in the dark I could see the blush in his cheeks.

"I'm glad to hear I've been memorable," I teased, putting an arm around his shoulder and pulling him in to nibble at the shell of his ear.

"Always, G. No matter whatever happens, the night sky will always be ours, okay?"

My stomach twisted and my heart sank at the implication of his words.

"What would happen, Jay? We're going to be together forever."

"I know, but just if."

"Don't talk like that," I insisted, squeezing him tighter to ward off the unimaginable if *he was speaking of. "There is no if. There's only the two of us, for-*

ever."

That memory has always been a sharp knife in the gut. It still is, but the pain is much duller now than it used to be. Now, I can hear Beck in the back of my mind, telling me it's not my fault, that I never could've known what was going through Johnny's mind at the time or that he needed help.

I watch as the sun creeps behind the horizon, the sky painted vibrant pinks and oranges, and I think of Beck. He said I needed to figure out how much of myself I could give him.

I know this past week without Beck has been near torture. I know I've fallen in love with him, even though I didn't think I was capable of loving anyone again. But Beck came into my life with his light and warmth, and he smoothed out the sharp, pointy parts inside of me and made me feel like myself again, like who I was before I was shredded.

But does all that mean I can let go of Johnny and give Beck everything he deserves?

I flop back and look up at the sky as the lights start to twinkle into existence in the darkening sky.

My blinks become long and slow as the chilly beach air swirls around me. I let out a contented sigh, and then I feel someone shift beside me.

I turn my head and I'm not at all surprised to see Johnny, looking at me with a dreamy smile.

"What are you doing here?"

Johnny lets out a quiet laugh. "I think the question is what are you doing here? You came here to talk to me, so let's talk."

I open and close my mouth, trying to come up with what I'm supposed to tell Johnny and how guilty I feel for falling in love with someone else.

Understanding dawns in Johnny's eyes, and he moves in for a kiss, but I turn my head at the last second, and his lips graze my cheek instead.

"I'm sorry," I murmur as he pulls back. "I still love you, it's just…"

"You don't belong to me anymore," he finishes knowingly. There's no bitter edge to his voice like I would've expected, just happiness and peace. "Don't be sad anymore, G. You were good to me, you loved me, and you gave me so many beautiful things to be grateful for. Now, let Beck give those things to you. You deserve everything good in the world, especially a man to share all the love I know you have to give."

My throat is too thick to speak, so I settle for a nod, choking back the tears that threaten to spill over.

"Can I ask one last favor?" Johnny asks, dipping his face a little and looking up at me through his eyelashes.

"Anything, Jay. For you, always anything."

"I never made it to senior prom, and I really wanted to slow dance with you."

I stand on shaky legs and hold my hand out to my first—but no longer my last—love. When he puts his hand in mine, I pull him toward me and into my arms. Regardless of Beck's lessons, I'm still a hopeless dancer, but I'm perfectly capable of holding Johnny close and swaying slowly in the moonlight to the music in our hearts.

"Thank you, G. You gave me everything, and I want all the happiness in the world for you. Promise me you'll be happy now."

"I promise. You can be at peace now; you don't have to worry about me anymore."

Johnny buries his face against my chest and nods. I close my eyes and enjoy the warm weight of him in my arms one last time.

"Goodbye, Jay."

"Bye." His voice fades as he dissipates in my arms.

"Sir, wake up." I startle awake to an authoritative voice and a bright light in my eyes. "You can't sleep here, you need to move it along."

"Sorry, I must've dozed off," I apologize, trying to shield my eyes from the light he's still shining on me.

I heave myself off the ground and attempt to brush some of the sand off, but that task seems to be hopeless, so I give up and head to my car.

I take a second to breathe once I'm in my car, and I notice a strange sense of peace that wasn't there before.

K M Neuhold

I don't know if Johnny's ghost just visited me in my dreams or if it was my own subconscious finally giving me permission to move on, but for the first time, I feel free. It seems possible to love Beck with my whole heart, even if Johnny will always be tattooed there as well.

Without checking the time, I pull my phone out and dial Beck.

"Hello?" he answers, sounding sleepy and confused.

"Hey, can I come over? I mean, I'm like an hour away, but when I get back to town, can I come over?" I ask in a rush, feeling an undeniable pull to be near Beck, to tell him how I feel, to run and scream that maybe it's possible to be put back together after you've been shattered. If the right person is there to show you how the pieces fit together.

"Is everything okay?" Beck suddenly sounds more alert and concerned.

"Everything is great," I assure him. "I just need to see you."

"Tonight isn't great, sweetie. I need a little time to think about things, and if you come over, I'll just get confused all over again."

My heart sinks.

"You don't want to see me anymore?"

"That's not it, Gage. But I don't think three in the morning is the time for this conversation. Why don't you come over after the sun is up and I've gotten my beauty rest? I'll make breakfast, and we can talk."

"Yeah, okay," I concede, a heavy weight settling in my heart.

"Gage, this isn't a fight, and nothing bad is going to happen to me, I promise. Okay?"

"Yeah," I agree, my heart giving a little squeeze at the understanding and concern Beck has for me. "Night."

"Night, babe."

I pound my fist hard against Adam's front door without regard for his neighbors or the fact that it's four in the morning.

The door flies open, and Adam stands there looking confused and concerned in nothing but a pair of boxers, his hair sticking up in every direction.

His eyes widen when he realizes I'm the one trying to bust down his door in the middle of the night.

"What's wrong? Did something happen to Beck?"

"I think he's breaking up with me," I lament. "He made me fall in love with him, and now he's going to leave me."

Sympathy dawns on Adam's face, and he steps aside to let me in.

Nox stumbles out of the bedroom, half

naked as well, rubbing his eyes.

"What's going on?"

I slump down on their couch and wonder why I came here to interrupt their sleep.

"All right, now why do you think Beck is breaking up with you?" Adam prompts, sitting down on the recliner beside the couch and letting Nox crawl into his lap. Nox rests his head against Adam's shoulder and seems to fall back to sleep.

"A week ago, he saw the picture of Johnny I have by my bed and he seemed jealous, which I totally get. I tried to tell him how serious I am about him and that I love him, but he cut me off and bolted. He's been avoiding me all week, and I've been a mess. I get what his fear is. He thinks I can never love him because I already gave my heart to Johnny. So tonight, I drove out to the beach to try to get my head on straight and figure out if Beck was right or not."

"And what did you figure out?" Adam prompts when I stop talking.

"It's like..." I struggle to find the words to describe how I feel about Beck and what he means to me.

"Like he's the missing piece of your heart?" Adam guesses, glancing down at Nox, snoring against his chest.

"No, it's better than that. It's more like, he's the picture on the puzzle box that shows me how my pieces are supposed to fit together."

Adam smiles, and I don't miss the relief in

his eyes. My heart gives a little twinge. I hadn't realized how much my isolation had hurt Adam to watch.

"Have you dreamed of Johnny since he died?" I ask abruptly. "Not like a normal dream, but where you felt as if you'd had a real conversation with him."

"A few times. The last one I had was a few months ago. We were sitting in my parent's kitchen table, and when I asked why he was there, he said I needed to talk to him. It was around the time you found out about Nox and me, so I ended up spilling my guts to Johnny about being bi and all the guilt I'd felt about hiding it. And I don't think I'll ever forget the way his words affected me. He said *I know. I know a lot of things now that I wish I'd known before.*"

I feel tears burning behind my eyes again. I choke them back and nod.

Beck said he thought some souls couldn't move on without closure. Jay has gotten his closure from Adam and from me now. I hope he can rest peacefully.

"Does he visit you often?" Adam asks cautiously.

"He used to. He won't be anymore, though. He said it's time we both move on. He wants me to be happy with Beck." My throat aches as I force the words out, but relief settles in my chest as I acknowledge out loud for the first time that it's truly time to move on.

CHAPTER 26

Beck

I'm pulled from a fitful sleep by the sound of my buzzer. I sit up and blink around at my surroundings.

Did Gage really call me in the middle of the night, his voice full of hope and excitement? Or was that nothing more than a wishful dream? God knows I've had enough dreams about Gage in the past few days and even one freaky one where I swear the same boy from the framed picture beside Gage's bed, Johnny, came to me and told me to love Gage hard and never let him go. It was an easy promise to make. I just wish I could believe Gage could give me the same. Maybe he can. Maybe that's what he called in the middle of the night to tell me.

I climb out of bed and go to find out who's buzzing me at an ungodly hour.

"Do you have any idea what time it is?" I grumble into the intercom.

"You said we could talk when the sun came up. The sun is up, now let me in."

My heart flips at the sound of Gage's voice. There's a new determination in it that I haven't heard before.

"Yeah, come on up." I push the button to unlock the door and then I unlatch my door and pull it open to wait for Gage as my heart rages behind my ribcage.

I hear him on the steps a few seconds later, and then he's standing in front of me, looking slightly worse for wear but every bit the man who owns my heart. How did I let that happen?

"Hey," I croak and then clear my throat before stepping aside to let Gage into my apartment.

"There's somewhere I want to take you."

"What? Baby, it's the crack of dawn; where could you possibly want to take me?"

"Please, Beck." Gage steps toward me with a look of pleading. "You told me I needed to think about how much I could give you and the answer, Beck, is everything. I can give you everything."

My heart jams in my throat as I try to figure out how his words can possibly be true. I want them so badly. I want Gage with everything in me, but I'm afraid to believe.

"How is that possible? Gage, the way you still feel for Johnny—"

Gage puts a hand over my mouth to stop my words.

"Just come with me?"

Gage

Beck is quiet as I drive us up to the bluff. My entire body is trembling with fear at the possibility Beck might still turn me away. He may never understand that I can love him and still have love in my heart for the man I lost. That won't ever mean the way I feel for Beck is diminished or halved.

When we reach the overlook I park and we both climb out of the car.

"This is a gorgeous view. Where are we?" Beck asks as he gazes out over the city from the high bluff.

"Johnny's favorite place. It was *our* place. We used to come here all the time together."

Beck stills at my words. "Why am I here?"

"Because I need you to understand. I loved Johnny so much. I loved him to the point of destruction. It wasn't his fault; it was mine because I couldn't let him go, and it shattered every part of me. But then you came along and put me back together. I don't know how to show you that I love you. But I swear to god, Beck, I do. I'll always love Johnny, but on my life, I love you more than I ever knew possible. Love isn't finite. You are tattooed all over the pieces of my heart, just like Johnny is. And, just like Johnny, I don't think I'll ever be able to let you go. I don't know if you noticed, but I'm not so good at half-assed."

"I did notice that," Beck agrees with a chuckle. He squints at me a little like he's trying to make sense of me, then he looks out over the city. "I don't ever want our love to shatter you the way your love for Johnny did."

"Then you'd better never leave me," I laugh.

"I guess I could live with that." Beck turns back to me and smiles. I hold my arms open, and he steps into them and looks up at me. "Is this the part where we ride off into the sunset for our happily ever after?"

"Since it's morning and I don't have a horse, would you settle for a spontaneous adventure instead?"

"Who are you, and what have you done with my broody tattoo artist?"

"I promise I'll do my best to get broody every once in a while, for you."

Beck laughs, and I'm overwhelmed by the urge to pull him closer and taste the sunshine on his lips. And I can, so I do.

There's no sense of urgency as I take my time savoring Beck's lush lips.

"So, where are we going?"

"I'm thinking we stop at our apartments and pack overnight bags and then jump in the car and head down the coast until we get somewhere warm enough that we can spend the weekend in a little bungalow with the windows wide open and a sea breeze trickling in as we stay naked and sweaty for a full forty-eight hours straight."

"Mmm, you really are the perfect man."

"Not perfect, just in love with someone who knows how all my pieces are supposed to fit together."

"I love you, too. I tried not to, but I don't

think it was ever in my control. My pieces need your pieces, and now we can both be whole and happy. And, most importantly, we can be to-gether."

"This is getting awfully sappy. I say we get moving so we can get a jump on the sweaty naked part."

Beck tells me to wait in the car while he packs a bag, insisting that I'll distract him if I come inside.

While I wait, I pull out my phone to call Adam so I can let him know not to worry about me being MIA for the weekend.

"How'd it go?" he asks as soon as he picks up the call.

I can't stop smiling; I'm fucking giddy. I may have even almost giggled at one point during the drive to Beck's place.

"So good," I confide. "We're taking off for the weekend, and I didn't want you to worry. I'll be back Monday for my appointments at the shop."

"That's fucking awesome. Go and enjoy, and if you need an extra day, I'll cover your appoint-ments. I'm just glad to hear you happy again."

"Me too." The door to Beck's building opens, and he flounces out. "Gotta go, I'll see you in a few days."

I hang up and then cock an eyebrow at Beck as he climbs into the car with only one small bag.

"I assumed I wouldn't be needing many clothes."

"God, I fucking love you." I can't stop saying it. I can't get over the way Beck's whole expression glows every time I do. And I may quickly become addicted to the electric current that runs through my body each time he says it back.

"I *am* extremely loveable," Beck agrees.

"Hey," I complain, reaching over the center console to tickle him.

"Mercy, no tickling. I love you too, you big bully."

Beck

I pinch my thigh for the third time to check if this day has been real.

Gage opens the door to our room and leads me in. We didn't manage to find a beach bungalow like he wanted, but we did get a room overlooking the beach. There's even large glass doors leading to a balcony right off the bedroom. It's perfect.

I toss my bag on the bed and pull open the balcony doors, taking a deep inhale of the salty sea air.

Gage's arms wrap around my middle from behind, and I melt into him with an excited shiver. Every single moment with Gage has been scorching hot, but I'd be lying if I said I wasn't excited to see what it will be like now that our emotions are all on the table.

His lips trail over the back of my neck and up to my ear where he licks and nibbles as my cock hardens.

I whimper when his mouth disappears.

"I need you naked, baby," Gage says, tugging on the bottom of my shirt.

I lift my arms and let him strip me. My pants are the next to go, this time taking my lace panties immediately with them.

Gage spins me around so I'm standing exposed before him, his eyes drinking me with an expression of unadulterated awe.

I return the favor and slowly rid Gage of his own clothes, kissing and caressing each bit of skin I uncover.

Gage stoops and grabs me by the backs of my thighs and lifts me up. I waste no time wrapping my legs around his hips and my arms around his neck.

Our lips find each other in a feverish dance of lips, tongues, and teeth.

I expect Gage to take me to the bed, but instead in a few short strides he has me pressed against the nearest wall.

My hands tangle in his hair as I kiss him harder, tasting the depths of his mouth as our aching erections rut against each other.

The room is filled with the sounds of our mixing breath and every desperate gasp and moan that falls from either of our lips.

"Hold on tight," Gage instructs.

He releases his grip on one of my thighs and shoves his hand between us, wrapping it around both our cocks.

"Oh fuck, yes," I gasp as Gage breaks away from my mouth to nip at my collar bone.

He jerks us faster as our pre-cum mixes and slicks the way. His rough mouth is everywhere at once, making my entire body tremble, my muscles taut.

Gage grunts as he thrusts his cock against mine, and I can feel as all his muscles pull tight at once, his shaft thick and ready to burst.

My head knocks back against the wall as a wave of pleasure crashes over me.

His hand stills, and I can feel our hot seed spilling over both of us.

Gage stumbles back, taking me with him as he collapses onto the bed. "I'll never get enough of you," he murmurs, cupping my face with his clean hand.

My heart stutters and swells as relief washes over me. Even without my high heels or lace, Gage still likes to have sex with me. It isn't about the kink. I could cry with relief. Instead, I settle for kissing him long and hard before getting us a towel to clean up and climbing into bed beside him.

Gage's thumb rubs a little circle over my ring finger as we watch the sun set through the window.

Our sweat slicked bodies stick together and our breathing synchronizes.

"I'm going to take that picture of Johnny out of the bedroom. Tell me where you're comfortable with having it and that's where it will go."

"Oh, sweetie, you don't have to do that."

I roll over so I'm facing him and run my hands along his chest and neck, wanting every bit of contact I can get.

"It made you leave," Gage argues in a strained voice, his expression vulnerable, his arms tightening around my waist.

"No, I left because I was freaked out, not because I was jealous or anything. I saw that picture, and for a second, I got my hopes up so high that maybe I'd found a man who could love me exactly as I am. But then reality hit me that you might never have that much emotion to offer. It scared me."

"Beck, please tell me you know now that I am absolutely crazy about everything you are."

"I do know. And thank you for that. I promise it's completely fine for you to leave the picture there."

"In fact, I think it's time to redecorate my whole place. Hell, maybe it will feel less empty if I get some color on the walls."

"You know what would feel even less lonely? Living with your boyfriend." As the words leave my lips, I know I'm only thirty percent joking. It's probably too soon, and no doubt, Gage is going to need to take things slow.

"Really?" Gage's eyes light with restrained hope.

"Only if the answer is yes, otherwise I'm totally joking."

"Smartass," he chuckles. "I'm in. Let's work out the logistics when we get home Monday. For now, the only thing I want to talk about is room service and blow jobs."

"I'm in. Anything involving you and me, I'm one hundred percent in."

"Careful, I might hold you to that."

"Whenever you're ready, the answer is yes."

"Good to know. Very good to know."

The End

MORE BY
K.M.NEUHOLD

The Heathens Ink Series

➢ Rescue Me (Heathens Ink, 1). To read this story about dealing with PTSD and addiction, and finding true love during an inconvenient time: click here

➢ Going Commando (Heathens Ink, 2). If you're looking for a lower angst story, you'll want to check out this sexy, fun friends-to-lovers with an epic twist! Get it Here

➢ From Ashes (Heathens Ink, 3). Don't miss this story about love in the face of deep physical and emotional scars: Click Here

➢ Shattered Pieces (Heathens Ink, 4). Grab this beautiful story about a feisty man who loves to wear lace and makeup trying his damndest to help a wounded soul heal: Click Here

➢ Inked in Vegas (Heathens Ink, 5) Join the whole crew for some fun in Las Vegas! Click HERE

➢ Flash Me (Heathens Ink, 6) Liam finally gets his men! Click HERE

The Heathens Ink Spin-off Series: Inked

➢ Unraveled (Inked, 1) And don't forget to read

the sexy, kinky friends to lovers tale! Click Here

➢ Uncomplicated (Inked, 2) Beau, the flirty bartender finally gets his HEA!

Replay Series

➢ If you missed the FREE prequel to the Replay series, get to know the rest of the band better! Click Here

➢ Face the Music (Replay, 1): click Here

➢ Play it by Ear (Replay, 2): click Here

➢ Beat of Their Own Drum (Replay, 3): Click Here

Ballsy Boys

Love porn stars? Check out the epic collaboration between K.M. and Nora Phoenix! Get a free prequel to their brand new series, and the first two books now!

➢ Ballsy (A Ballsy Boys Prequel). Meet the men who work at the hottest gay porn studio in L.A. in this FREE prequel! Click Here

➢ Rebel (Ballsy Boys, 1) If anyone can keep it casual it's a porn star and a break-up artist. Right?? Click Here

➢ Tank (Ballsy Boys, 2) Don't miss this enemies to lovers romance that will set your Kindle on fire! Click Here

➢ Heart (Ballsy Boys, 3) Like a little ménage action with your porn stars? Don't miss bad boy porn star Heart falling for not only his nerdy best friend, Mason, but also his own parole officer, Lucky! Click Here

➢ Campy (Ballsy Boys, 4) a sexy cowboy and a porn star with secrets! Grab Campy's story now! Click Here

Working Out the Kinks

➢   Stay (Working Out The Kinks, 1) What happens to a couple when one of them discovers a kink he's not so sure his partner will be into? Enjoy this super cute, low-angst puppy play story! Click Here

Stand-Alone Shorts

➢   Always You- A super steamy best friends to lovers short! A post-college weekend, a leaky ceiling, and a kiss they weren't expecting. Click Here

➢   That One Summer- A Young Adult story about first love and the one summer that changes everything. Click Here

➢   Kiss and Run- A 30k steamy, Valentine's Day novella. Click Here

ABOUT THE AUTHOR

Author K.M.Neuhold is a complete romance junkie, a total sap in every way. She started her journey as an author in new adult, MF romance, but after a chance reading of an MM book she was completely hooked on everything about lovely- and sometimes damaged- men finding their Happily Ever After together. She has a strong passion for writing characters with a lot of heart and soul, and a bit of humor as well. And she fully admits that her OCD tendencies of making sure every side character has a full backstory will likely always lead to every book having a spin-off or series. When she's not writing she's a lion tamer, an astronaut, and a superhero...just kidding, she's likely watching Netflix and snuggling with her husky while her amazing husband brings her coffee.

STALK ME

Website: authorkmneuhold.com
Email: kmneuhold@gmail.com
Instagram: @KMNeuhold
Twitter: @KMNeuhold
Bookbub
Join my Mailing List for special bonus scenes and teasers!
Facebook reader group- Neuhold's Nerds You want to be here, we have crazy amounts of fun

Made in United States
Orlando, FL
17 May 2022

17962503R00146